IF I COULD SLEEP

ALEX B. STONE

IF I COULD SLEEP

RED HEIFER PRESS

IF I COULD SLEEP, a novel by Alex B. Stone.
Copyright © 2004 by Alex B. Stone
First Edition
Published in the United States by Red Heifer Press,
P.O. Box 1891, Beverly Hills, California 90213-1891.
All rights reserved.

Cover design by Jorge A. Pringles (L.A. Press)
Typesetting and book design by Red Heifer Press.

Library of Congress Control Number: 2004090281
ISBN: 0-9631478-6-2

Acknowledgments

"Self-Portrait" by Hans Burkhardt (Basel, 1904 - Los Angeles, 1994), courtesy of Jack Rutberg Fine Arts, Los Angeles, and the Hans G. & Thordis Burkhardt Foundation. Digital Photography by Jack Rutberg.

For Martha My Love

Chapter One

Only three more mornings of Fred you still have so much to be
thankful for. Sunday my little sister Helen will fly back to her New
York home—back to bridge on Monday, book club on Tuesday,
museum docent on Wednesday, golf on Sunday.

Helen sits in the rocker. "What do you want for supper, Fred? I'll
make you anything you want."

Helen is watching me, the widowed mourning father. Helen is
making pleasant trills again. "I am so pleased you don't mind living
alone. You should let Mrs. Bixbe cook for you."

I nod, close my eyes. Nothing stops Helen.

"You don't do anything about changing your life, Fred. You sit
here all alone in this big house. When Dotty died it was the same
thing. You just sat there, agreed to everything, changed nothing."

First Dotty, in the autoaccident. Now, eight years later, Emily,
dead in an avalanche. I was always against spring skiing. Emily was in
Vienna to attend the Colloquium on Feline Leukemia Virus. Stupid of
Emily to die in the Austrian Alps on Easter Sunday morning. First, I
lose a wife, then a child.

And Helen, again . . .

"Fred, you have so much to be thankful for. You still have two
daughters who love you." I nod yes to Helen.

"Fred, how about veal chops, mashed potatoes and dark beer, like Mama used to make?"

Helen is a better cook than our mother ever was. But then the Sterns were a family of luftmentshen—intellectuals, philosophes. Mama was not educated by her tutors to be a hausfrau or whatever they call a housewife in Polish. Mama was a woman who read Sienkiewicz and passed out revolutionary pamphlets. Down with the Czar! Helen . . . well, Mama did not do veal chops.

Philosophes was what our Uncle Charlie called our mother and father. Philosophes, in their Yiddish, meant immigrant intellectuals who can't earn a living. Not even in this land of opportunity. Mama had to sew lamp shades, Papa swept the floors of his brotherinlaw's factory. It was that brotherinlaw who brought us out of Poland. Brought us from what would have become assured death to this Golden Land of freedom.

"Fred, you still have a lot to be thankful for."

Helen. Pollyanna. Helen sitting in the corner doing her needlepoint, doing her good deed, her deed of lovingkindness for me, the living brother; for Emily, the dead niece. Helen with her round smile in her round face with the palest blue eyes. Helen should lose weight, take up exercise. Swimming would help her arthritis.

"The neighbors left enough food for weeks. Maybe we should use some of the food that is in the freezer."

"You can eat that frozen stuff when I am not here to cook for you. I'll make an inventory of what is in the freezer, then I'll write down the length of time you will need in the microwave for it to thaw."

"Helen, I don't use the microwave."

"The microwave is clean and quick."

"I put the packets in the stove like Dotty used to do."

"I'll bet Dorothy used the microwave. You just didn't know it. I'll show you how. I'll show you tomorrow. For lunch I'll thaw some of the lasagna Eva brought."

"Eva's lasagna is awful. I'd rather make a cheese sandwich."

"You'll have plenty of time to eat cheese sandwiches.

"What are you going to do with your days, Fred? Why don't you come out, spend a month with us on the Cape? The weather in Rockville is awful. April fifteenth. Still cold and raining."

"It's not cold, it's forty five degrees."

"It's cold. Depressing and cold."

Helen, you too would have gotten used to it like Dotty and I did. You can get used to anything you have to, Helen. Of course, you never had to—not since you married George Gordon.

"Life with George has made you soft."

"Marrying George Gordon was the best thing I ever did. I would still be sitting here in Rockville dreaming of a weekend in Chicago and two weeks in Florida in January."

"You know, Helen, the Art Institute has the Magritte exhibition."

"I saw it in New York. Remember? I wrote and told you. I sent you the catalog."

"You're right. So you did."

"Fred, you still have a lot to be thankful for. Edna and Edith are loving, caring daughters. Not everyone has such caring children. Edna told me she would love to have you live with her. And don't give me that I have my life she has her life. What sort of a life is it for you here in Rockville? You go to morning services. You go down to the Y, swim a little, have lunch with your cronies. The same buddies you have been having lunch with for twenty years. What can you talk about for twenty years?"

"Thirty years."

"Okay, thirty years. A man of your intelligence, Fred, you should move to Chicago. You don't want to live with Edna live close to her. Meet new people. You have always been interested in art."

"I read the catalogs."

"There are lectures at the Art Institute. Join a synagogue that has an adult education program."

Helen the culture maven. Helen who did succeed, did get out of Rockville, did educate herself in matters cultural and artistic and aesthetic.

"Sell your office building, sell this house. Live a little."

"I have learned to live alone."

"You don't have to live alone. You are a young man."

"A seventy year old young man with an arthritic spine."

"You can find a better life in Winnetka . . ."

Helen never stops rocking, never drops a stitch. Never stops.

"I think I'll go lie down for a while. I didn't sleep so well last night."

"Nobody our age sleeps well, Fred. Fred, I'm not going to let you sleep for more than an hour. You sleep more than an hour you won't sleep tonight. That's true, I heard that on teevee—the medical station. It wouldn't do you a bit of harm if we watched a little teevee tonight. Since when are you so religious that you can't watch Mystery? That's like reading a book. If you wouldn't ask the Rabbi if it was all right for you to read a mystery book why can't we watch Mystery?"

Helen and George are always right. Their success, their wealth prove it. So I fritter away my days in Rockville on the Mississippi where the river runs from east to west. Here, you are needed. Here you are a big man, Fred. The Tenth Man.

"Here I am part of the miracle that we still have a minyan for morning prayers."

"The Rockville Jewish Center will survive without you."

"I have my life, my routines. The days go smoothly, quickly. It's Monday, it's Friday, it's Saturday afternoon. My afternoon naps, then Brad and I walk along the river."

"What do you and Brad talk about? He is twenty years younger than you."

"We discuss symbolism in late nineteenth century American

writing. Writers are good readers and Brad writes very well."

"If Brad is such a fine writer, how come I never heard of him?"

"I tell you, Helen, Brad writes very well."

"All you know about writing, Fred Stern, is what you read in the New York Times. You spend all Sunday reading the Times Book Review. Then you do a little yard work. Why don't you hire your yard work done? A man of your means. Fred, what are you saving your money for? You give money to Edna, you give money to Edith. They don't need your money. Spend it on yourself, make your life easier."

"My life would have been different if Dotty hadn't died."

"If, Fred. You remember what Mama said? If Grandma had wheels she would have been a trolley car.

"You had to go into Dorothy's dad's one truck building business. Fred, you could have had a great career teaching economics. Your classmates have won Nobel prizes."

"Helen, in our first twenty years our construction company earned more money than four Nobel Laureates earn in forty years and that's giving them full credit for their prize money."

"Fred, you haven't driven a nail in years. In the ten years you've managed property you have lost forty percent of your assets. The longer you stay in business, the worse off you are."

"We have an obligation to our employees."

"Fred, if there is no profit, you can quit, give up. Stop bleeding."

"Lack of profitability is not my fault. That's a market condition. I run a clean shop, pay decent wages."

"That's what all you building contractors say until you get indicted for labor law violations or for safety code violations. How did your IRS case come out? You paid plenty, didn't you, Fred?"

"I never got a chance to tell our side of the story. I was intimidated into paying. I was paying attorneys to defend our position. Three years later it was cheaper to settle. Every one of the civil fraud charges was dropped. That was part of the settlement."

"If the IRS had no basis for claiming fraud, they wouldn't have brought the civil fraud charges against you, Fred. That's what George told me."

"My dear sister, civil fraud charges are brought to intimidate you so that the IRS can assess penalties against the innocent taxpayer. Helen, I am going to lie down for a few minutes. You are in full charge. I didn't sleep well last night."

"You could take a sleep aid."

Now my sister is practicing medicine.

"If you slept at night you wouldn't be so damn tired in the mornings. You wouldn't be napping your afternoons away. Okay, go take your nap if you can't keep your eyes open. I'll wake you in a half hour."

Thank you, Helen, thank you. What do we say from Psalm 30 in the morning prayers? Weeping may tarry for the night, but joy comes in the morning. How can I have joy in the mornings? First Dotty gets killed and now Emily. Both dead.

Forty years ago—no, fortythree!—I joined Harris Construction. When Dotty and I were married. Sam was building fine singlefamily homes. Anyone can build, Sam. That is, any one with hands like yours. Sam was from the old school. Apprenticed at fourteen. Hardworking and honest. Had golden hands, did beautiful work. Other contractors came to admire his stairs. Until I came along and married his daughter all Sam ever made was wages.

You know what increases profit, Sam? The financing. What you pay for money, Sam. Money is a commodity. You buy it well, you make more profit.

From this I don't know. From building I know. I never went to college, Fred. So now it's not good enough to build a quality home at a fair price?

Sam, it is not good enough to make a small profit when you can make a big profit.

Alex B. Stone

The water is dripping off the roof. Drip, drop, plunk. I can't sleep at night, can't nap. Can't keep the window open because of the spring sounds. The woodpecker is at the red oak again. Latest spring in my memory. Yesterday there was a barnswallow clinging to the garage wall. Too bewildered, too confused to find its way out of an open garage. That's the way life is, Fred, you see only the wall. You don't realize there is a way out to the right, light to the left.

The way out is up into the light.

What are you going to do about that, Fred?

Nothing. Nothing at all.

Chapter Two

"You feeling better, Fred? Did you sleep?"

"I was looking at Emmy's Bat Mitzvah pictures."

Fred, your bedroom is a picture gallery. It's time to put Emmy and Dotty's photos in the albums. Fred, your bedroom is a shrine. Dotty is gone, Emmy is buried, you don't need photos of the dead staring at you from the top of your dresser.

"I heard you talking in there. Were you talking to Dorothy and Emily? To me it sounded like you were complaining about something. There are many that are a lot worse off than you, Fred Stern."

"I don't talk to myself and I wasn't complaining."

Those photos, Helen, are memories of joyous occasions. Of when we were together. A family.

Dotty Harris was one of the bestlooking girls in Rockville. Tall, thin, red hair and green eyes, small breasts and small hips. The Harrises were all goodlooking.

All gone. Dotty's brother Jack dead at twentyfive. Jack had a good head. Cancer doesn't discriminate. Good head, bad head. If Jack hadn't died, he would have come into the business. I could have retired, done anything I wanted. I would have completed my Rockville Tales. It takes more than 150 pages of stories to make a collection. That, Fred B. Stern, is fifteen or twenty stories. You, Fred, have written six stories in six years.

Brad thinks well of my writing.

Brad can't get his own stories published. Why should any one read Fred B. Stern's perspective on life in Western Illinois?

That's what I'll do. I'll start sending my stories out to the little literary magazines.

No one is interested in stories of crisis and confrontation in the world of small business. Have you ever read a story in The New Yorker that deals with business ethics or partnership conflicts or confrontations with the IRS?

I can write about love, commitment and middleage.

Fred, you are a bit more than middleaged. You are past seventy. I can only write about what I understand.

You could write about Worldwar II and Korea. That would be of greater interest than slices of life in Rockville or changing traditions in a small midwestern conservative Jewish congregation. Fred, there is no market for death and disability and aging. Genre is where it's at. You want to publish? Write mystery, write romance, write scifi.

"Fred, do you hear me? I made a tunafish casserole. You like noodles. What time do you want lunch?"

"It's only eleven, Helen."

"So? You won't be going swimming for the next three days—I must say, though. You have been swimming at noon for forty years. Your cronies know you're at home sitting Shiva. Have they come by to console you? No, they send flowers."

"It's not a Christian tradition to call at the bereaved's home."

"Don't apologize for your friends, Fred. They could have at least called.

"I wasn't apologizing."

"Anyway, it's not so very Christian of them. They could have at least called. By the way, I forgot to tell you, a Don Belsky called. A man with a big booming voice and a strange manner. I told him you were resting. I wrote down what he said. You get him up! You tell Fred Stern I called and I am not going to call him again. He wants to do business with me, he can call me. You enjoy that kind of company, Fred? What kind of a man would call you at home during your mourning week?"

"Harold Belsky's son."

"Like father, like son. You remember? Harold would promise you everything and deliver nothing. But still—talking that way to me—and you in mourning!"

It's my fault. Should have been more careful. Shouldn't have done business with him. But Donald came to me. I said no, then I said no again. Wore me down. It's my fault. Contract should have been more explicit. But that was five years ago. Don't want to do any more business with Donald Belsky—just can't get rid of him. Fred Stern, the crabby old landlord taking advantage of poor Donald Belsky, the innocent tenant. Fred, you need this? I don't need it, it just won't go away. Don owes us and he won't pay. If Don weren't Jewish, I'd see him in small claims court. Sue him to break the lease, throw him out. How does it look, Fred Stern, a man who goes to morning prayers sues another Jew over a couple of thousand dollars?

"Helen, you don't understand. That's the Belsky tactic. Donald calls me at home. He knows I won't talk to him. Now he is the good guy—he is offering to settle, to pay what he owes us—if I extend the lease. So, now Donald can tell everyone in the congregation, I offered to pay Fred Stern! Fred wouldn't take my money. Fred won't extend my lease."

"What kind of person would do that to a father in mourning for his child?"

Emmy was fortytwo. Not a child, not a married woman. A career woman, a professional woman too busy to get married.

Papa, you don't understand. I don't want to get married. I don't need children. Edith needs children. Dotty had asked, Is learning to fly more important than learning to live with a husband?

I know, Mama. When I am a lonely old maid living alone just me and my dog and two cats, my sisters will be surrounded by their loving adoring children.

Papa, Mama, I want to go to Kansas State Veterinary School like Grandpa did.

If that is what you want, Emmy.

That's what I want.

About a month after Emmy got settled in Manhattan she invited us to visit.

There is something I want to show you.

What is it, Emmy?

A surprise for you and Mom.

Dorothy thought Emmy had met a young man.

Dotty, if Emmy had a young man she would tell you on the phone.

So what is all the mystery about?

We'll find out . . .

Iowa Interstate 80 West is construction, detours, tractortrailers and graintrucks hauling corn to be dried; to be stored; to be shipped to Russia. The John Deere green machine cornpicker swallows the browned, dried rows of corn, coughs, spits the corn kernels into the grain trucks.

Dotty sleeps in the seat beside me. The sun shines bright. In Marysville, Nebraska, south of Lincoln, we stop for a donut and coffee, then south through the Flint Hills, past the lake. By the dam we descend into the Kaw River Valley.

If you come before 5, I'll meet you at the Veterinary school.

It was about 4:30 when I parked by the Basic Science building, found a smiling Emmy in the microbiology lab.

My surprise. Follow me.

Emmy led us through the waiting room of the small animal clinic. Cats and meows on the left, dogs and barks on the right. By a row of administrative offices: Dean, Assistant Dean . . . Then, halfway down another hallway, a space of grey wall and, beneath a festoon of purple letters (the Kansas State color), Donors to Veterinary Medicine, a faded eightbytwelve blackandwhite photo of my motherandfather—younger than I remember them. Papa standing straight, eyes front, without the grey moustache with which he chose to adorn his middleandold age. Mother, almost as tall, beside him.

That afternoon Emmy was so proud and pleasant.

Papa, do you know that the dean knew that I was Dr. Benjamin Stern's granddaughter? You know what the dean said? You look like your grandpa. That, of course, is silly. I really look like Grandma.

Emmy certainly did look like Mama. Tall and thin. Maybe that's why I married Dorothy Harris. Because she looked like my mother.

Once someone met your grandpa there were few that would forget him is what I said. Then Dotty asked, Are you happy, Emmy?

Yes, Mama.

That's all I wanted to hear.

That was one advantage we gave our daughters. A good midwestern small liberalarts college education. Not one of our daughters prattles in the bigcity intellectual chic language of the headworkers. All three took advanced degrees, but I am always thankful that they didn't join the Birkenstock sandal brigades.

You know what Grandpa always said: Where but in America could a Jewish immigrant get an opportunity to work his way through veterinary school? Grandpa thought that was such a special favor, but I found out something about Grandpa's class—why Grandpa was admitted that year. He thought it was the college that gave him his opportunity.

Of course, it did.

Yes and no, Dad. That year there were not enough Kansas applicants to fill the class, so they took Grandpa from Brooklyn. Had there been more Kansans who wanted to go to veterinary school,

Grandpa would have been out. Kansas law required that Kansas residents receive first choice. Preferred entry.

Emmy laughed. Now it's all reversed. I got preference because Grandpa was an old grad who had supported his college most generously.

All Papa ever wanted to do was veterinary medicine. He froze in the Illinois winters, sweated through the Illinois summers. He vaccinated hogs until his asthma got so advanced that three desensitization injections a week could no longer stop his wheezing, whooping. Even if Papa wore a dustmask he couldn't breathe in the hoglots.

My father and mother's wedding picture stands on the shelf above my bed.

"Helen, would you like Mama and Papa's wedding picture? I could make a copy of it for you for your grandchildren."

It's the grandchildren who concern themselves with their grandparents. It was Emmy who asked what was it like to be a country vet. It was Emmy who used to say, I'll bet you were the best veterinarian in Rock County. My father would smile, twinkle his green eyes. There weren't very many of us then . . .

"Lunch, Fred. Time to quit your writing."

"I have a paragraph to move."

"Move your paragraph, Fred."

Chapter Three

"Say something, Fred. I went to a lot of trouble so that you can have a hot lunch."

"I'll be right there."

Thank you, Helen. Thank you so much. Now I am the beneficiary of the hot lunch program for the bereaved.

"Fine tuna casserole, Helen. Thank you."

A day early.

Dotty's Thursday dinner, tuna casserole or cheese blintzes. Thursday was our light supper because that was my day for business lunches.

"Fred, you were up half the night."

"I had trouble sleeping."

It rained all night. Not hard, just enough for me to hear the water rattling down the drain.

"You'll sleep better once . . ."

"I haven't slept well since Dotty died."

"No one ever died from insomnia."

I wish I could die for three, four hours, just to get a bit of rest. Death is all or nothing, Fred. You know that.

"You look tired, Fred."

"I go to bed tired, wake up tired."

"You could ask Dr. Gold to give you a sleep aid."

"Sleeping pills make me stupid. Last one I tried I was dulled until two o'clock of the next afternoon."

"You are going to be at home for the next three days. Tonight, I'll give you half of my pill. See how you feel the next day."

"I get the most awful dreams with sleeping pills."

"So you lose a morning. The rest will do you good."

The cardinals and finches are back. I'll have to refill their feeders.

"Will you try to help yourself, Fred? You don't try to help yourself! Tea or coffee? Fred?"

"I'll have a glass of milk."

"I'm making a hot drink for myself. It's no trouble."

"Coffee."

"Have you learned to make coffee yet?"

"I have. Instant espresso. One and a half heaping demitasse spoons of dehydrated coffee, add boiling water."

"Fred, do you want me to make a real espresso for you? You don't use the espresso machine. Fred, that is a made in Switzerland espresso maker and you keep it covered up under wraps."

"Dotty used the machine."

For me, the instant is good enough, nothing to clean. Just rinse the china, the spoon, ready for the next time.

"Your demitasse cup and saucer are the most beautiful French china I have ever seen."

"Dotty bought the china, Emily, the espresso maker."

When the forsythia began to bud, I would cut some of the twigs, bring them into the house, force the yellow blossoms for Dotty's early spring.

"I found two dead Viburnum that will have to be replaced."

"I thought you had a mild winter."

"Everything on God's earth is finite, Helen. Death determined by a biological clock unless there is an accident and then death comes sooner."

"All you do is talk about death."

"Death and taxes."

"Talking of taxes, Fred, did you notice how much the taxes went up on the condo?"

"Sanibel is an upmarket location, Helen."

"George and I only use the condo two weeks a year."

"You own half."

"George was wondering if you would consider selling."

"That wasn't the folks' idea when they left it to us."
Sanibel was where our families would meet, be together, spend time together.

"Our Rachel isn't going to come from Paris to spend two weeks in Florida with . . ."

". . . her Uncle and cousins."

"I didn't mean that. I meant I think we should sell."

"You and George want to sell, I'll buy your half and then you and George can come and be my guests."

"I didn't mean it like that. It's just with all the maintenance expenses going up and up and with us living in New York . . ."

"I know. Why would you want to come to Florida to be with me and my daughters."

"You know how busy George is."

"You have time to go to Europe, but you can't find the time to come to Rockville unless there is a funeral."

"Don't be so peevish, Fred. Why would I want to come to Rockville?"

"To visit the graves of your parents."

If I Could Sleep . . .

"You are the keeper of the shrines, Fred."

You got the house, you got the tree farm, you got half the condo. With that, you get the graveyard.

The Viburnum along the fence line have to be pruned. The lawn under the oaks has to be reseeded. The logging road on the farm has to be cleared or we won't be able to get down to the creek.

"It's been a bad spring for floods, Helen. Worst in ten years."

"Fred, you can't worry about everything."

"Should get the creek cleaned out or it will dam up."

"That won't hurt anything, Fred. Leave it alone. Now you have Emmy's estate on your hands. Sell out, Fred. Enjoy. Fred, you really have enough to do with settling Emmy's affairs. Why don't you seriously try to get out of your business problems?"

"It's good advice, Helen. I know George wants his money out of my development company. If we sell some of the lots, I'll pay George."

"We aren't getting any younger, Fred. At the rate you are selling those lots, we'll never get paid out."

"Never is a long time, Helen. George has gotten his interest."

"Twelve years is a long time, Fred."

"No market, no sales."

"Fred, you have to get rid of your problems."

"Helen, my boiled water espresso is hotter than the espresso you made with the machine."

"No it isn't. And mine is better tasting. Admit it, Fred."

"We should have quite a few callers this evening."

"I have enough cake, don't worry. Your sister will make a good impression."

"People still ask for you, Helen."

"That's Rockville, Fred. Nothing has changed in forty years."

"I wouldn't say that, Helen."

"Sure, half of the congregation has died and all the young people left."

"Some come back for the Holy Days."

"If they went to Chicago they do."

Never expected Helen to come back to Rockville. Not after she has seen New York. Symphony, Art, Music. The big difference in Rockville in forty years? The railroad is gone. Dotty and I would go up to Chicago on the morning train. Breakfast in the diner. Two and a half hours later we are on La Salle Street. The Art Institute in the morning, lunch at Berghoff's, matinee at the Shubert, dinner at the Palmer House. What was the name of their supper club? The Empire Room! We heard Piaf there. Piaf, a small black figure backed by six big men in black.

Black was the color of my true love's hair.

"What did you say, Fred?"

"I said it's too cold to sit outside."

"Whom are you expecting tonight?"

"The Rabbi will come, the Hazzan, Dr. Gordon . . . you remember Dr. Gordon? and Herman Gottwalt. You'll recognize Herman. He is eighty five, hasn't changed in twenty years. Doesn't look a day over seventy. And Bill Katz, you remember Bill?"

"Your buddy who was a naval pilot?"

"That's Bill."

"As good looking as ever?"

"You won't have any trouble recognizing him."

"In our congregation no one sits Shiva."

"It's a fine tradition."

"That's Rockville. Forty years of tradition. I walk into the synagogue for Emmy's funeral, it's the same faces, the same service."

"It's a different rabbi. Things have changed. We now count women for the morning Minyan and women can come up to read from the Torah."

"For all this, we thank you."

If I Could Sleep . . .

"It's a step, Helen."

"Not even half a step, Fred. I saw the cemetery. Nothing has changed there. A row for women, a row for men."

"Emily is buried next to her mother."

"When are you going to have family plots so that we can all be together?"

"I can take it up with the cemetery board."

"You know what you'll get, Fred. You the big giver give the congregation thousands and what do you get when you asked that Emmy's funeral be in the sanctuary? No, Mr. Stern. No funerals in the synagogue. Poor Emily. So young. She did accomplish so much in her short life.

I loved you, Emmy. Did you know I loved you? Did you find someone to love you, Emily, when you left home? You were our oldest, Emmy, our firstborn. It took your mother and me a while to understand that you wouldn't marry, there would be no grandchildren. You were grandpa's girl until you were fifteen, sixteen. Really, until you left home and went to the University. What did you discover at the University of Illinois? Feminism? Equal opportunity? We lost you for those four years until you went to veterinary school. Your obituary will be six or eight lines in the Journal of the American Veterinary Medical Association. Emily Harris Stern (KSU '76) 42, Denver, Colorado, died April 23, 1993. Dr. Stern was a general practitioner with a special interest in feline infectious diseases. After graduating from KSU, Dr. Stern was a postdoctoral fellow at the Cornell University Feline Virus Research Center. In 1980, she established the Mountain View Veterinary Center in Denver, Colorado. Dr. Stern was a member of AVMA. Memorials may be made to the Kansas State University College of Veterinary Medicine student loan fund.

When Papa died I called Emily in Champaign. Emily didn't cry. She asked, Dad, when is Grandpa's funeral? I told her, Tomorrow at ten a.m. She said, I'll be there.

Alex B. Stone

After the rabbi's eulogy, Emily stood up and began to speak and smile. Why she smiled, I don't know. My grandfather always tried to do the right thing. He was the only man I knew who treated everyone the same way. Child or adult, he gave them a story, a smile, encouragement and reminiscences.

When I was a little girl—I must have been five or six—I was riding with Grandpa on his morning calls. It had to have been early in the spring because all Grandpa did that morning was pull out dead calves from bellowing, crying cows, and I asked Grandpa, Papa, don't you ever get a live calf? Papa didn't answer then, but, on the drive back, I'll never forget what my Papa told me. Emmy, he said, I remember every dead horse, every dead cow, every calf, every dog that died under my care. That was when I asked, Papa, why were the calves dead? The farmers waited too long to call for help. You can't blame the farmer. He hopes the cow will calve without a veterinarian's bill. The calves aren't worth all that much, so he waits too long. Then I asked, Grandpa, doesn't the cow hurt when she is not able to have her calf? And Papa said, Emmy, birth pain is part of the pain of life, of giving life. And then Papa laughed, Papa said, I always give the cow a spinal anesthetic. By the time I come to help, that poor cow has had enough pain for that year. Papa knew about pain.

Then Emmy sat down, took my mother's hand in hers, put it to her cheek and kissed her hand.

"George says it's not easy to sell a veterinary clinic."

"We'll see, Helen. I'll find out soon enough."

"It's a shame Emmy never got married."

It was after Emmy's graduation from Veterinary School she sat us down in the coffee shop of the Manhattan Holiday Inn. Dad, I am not made for marriage and children. I know I am a disappointment to you and mother. You want grandchildren to hug and to hold. You want pictures of blueeyed, loving children to share with your friends.

Emmy was a very active child. Blueeyed with darkcurly hair. She ran, ran, ran, her diaper coming down, Dotty after her and our Boston terrier yipping at both.

After Papa died, I think Emily went to see a therapist at the University clinic. I can't recall whether she told us then or if we found out years later. Emmy didn't show her grief, not to Dotty and me. She went right back into her studies.

That summer she taught tennis at the countryclub and began her flying lessons. Every penny she made that summer she spent on flying. By then she had the money Grandpa left her.

Give her the gun. Way up high in the sky . . . Papa sang the airforce songs of World War II and Emmy sang with him. Hand in hand, Emmy and Papa, into the hoglots of Western Illinois. Emmy sitting on the rail fence, her feet dangling, Papa examining the piglets. The sow felt threatened, tried to bite Emily's toes. Papa slapped his gloved hand to the sow's nose. Emmy laughs and laughs when she tells me. Papa saved me. The sow wanted to eat me up! She laughs and laughs when she tells her Papastories at supper.

"Fred?"

"Yes?"

"When are you going to Denver? Do you want George to help you? To meet you in Denver?"

The Austrian hotelier, so deferential, so polite with just the right amount of concern. Of course. I will arrange everything. The body must not be embalmed. Wrapped in a sheet. Yes, of course, I understand, the Mosaic laws, of course. A whitepine box, sealed, with wooden handles.

Emmy's clothes perfectly packed by an assistant manager into her twentyfour inch case. Underwear and nightgown under, a blue wool turtleneck, one rustcolored silk dress, a denim skirt, two pairs of shoes, a swim suit, a sweat suit. Emmy's ski clothes, cleansed of blood immediately after the accident, in a plastic sack, all identified for customs. Austrian Air Lines to New York, American Air Lines to Rockville, Illinois. The customs declaration signed and attested to by A. Horst & Sons, Vienna, Austria, Undertakers since 1912.

"Fred, what are you going to do about Emmy's estate? Do you want George to file the IRS forms for you?"

"Emmy's girlfriend is an attorney in town. I think Emily would have wanted her to handle her affairs."

Smalltown attorneys.

Smalltown attorneys aren't competent to handle large estates.

"What are you going to do with Emmy's airplane? Sell it? Airplanes are such drains. George says he doesn't know why anyone would want to own an airplane or a boat. If you want the use of one rent it is what George tells his clients."

I'm not going to take flying lessons. If Emmy wanted an airplane, so what? She didn't take from anyone, she didn't have children to support. Just she and her airplane. Emmy didn't buy the plane until she gave up supporting her trotters.

I hope Emmy left enough cash to pay the estate taxes.

Helen wants to know how large an estate Emily left. Helen or George or both have done their quick analytical addition. Add the value of Emmy's condo in Vail to her condo in Denver, the BMW, the airplane, Papa's money that she invested, plus the value of the veterinary practice at six times earnings, and then the value of the real estate is how George would do it, and that means that Emmy's estate will require 300thousand dollars in cash to settle the taxes. The IRS won't wait.

"Fred, close the door. I'm cold."

It's a late spring. Another week of rain. The magnolias should have been out by now, the cornplanting is late. We can't switch to beans. We had beans last year. We'll have to take our chances with corn.

I'll have to get the contractor who put in the drainage ditch on the north boundary of the farm to come back, to return the dirt he piled up between our cornfield and the road to the cornfield. He created a dam when he put in the ditch. Now our fields can't drain dry. I have called him twice, written a letter. The contractor used our topsoil to fill the ditch. That is why we have a lake in the cornfield.

Good luck Fred, on getting your cornfield repaired.

You were a good neighbor, Fred. You gave permission for the ditch to be put in along your boundary line. The heavy construction machinery was not to go onto the cornfield. I have photos of the caterpillar tracks across the cornfield. Go to it, Fred, fight. Fight to restore your cornfield. Even if you succeed it will be too late to put in a crop. Good fences make good neighbors. All the Jews are rich, so the contractor borrowed Fred Stern's topsoil. That's easier, cheaper than trucking in the fill. The Jews can afford it!

"Fred, what were you doing outside?"

"I went to smell the viburnum."

"That Viburnum at your front door must be forty years old. I can never smell a thing out there."

It was 33 years ago that I replanted that viburnum. I brought it from our first house. When we built in Oak Hills. Emily was the only one of our daughters in school. She adjusted so well to her new school. We wanted to be closer to the Jewish Center, close to Papa and Mama. When Papa retired he took up morning prayers—not that Papa became more religious just because he went to morning prayers from Monday to Friday. On Saturday and Sunday the working folks can go is what Papa said. Being part of the Minyan was Papa's payback to the community. Papa felt it was his very presence that made it possible for the daily memorial prayers to be recited—the Kaddish—the Torahportions to be read on Mondays and Thursdays. Papa wasn't convinced of the wisdom of the Torah until he began studying Talmud. Think of it, Fred. According to the Rabbis of the Talmud, meat from cattle with injury to the spine has been forbidden to us from the time of Moses.

Papa took from his religion what he wanted, left the rest easily. I remember Papa's I don't eat pork and I don't eat nonkosher beef and I don't eat shellfish and I won't eat catfish. For me that works, but what someone else does, that's not for me to judge. Deeds of lovingkindness, Fred, that's where it's at.

We never saw Emmy in her coffin. I wanted to see her, but I knew Dotty wouldn't have permitted me to view our pale white firstborn in her decay and death. How could I be sure it was Emily in that coffin? It could be another young woman. Maybe she was skiing with someone and their identities were mistaken, switched?

Dr. Stern was alone in a single room with the view of our mountain lakes. The very best room.

Maybe Emily was with someone who did not spend the nights with her. The photograph on her passport is a very good likeness.

I gave Dr. Stern's passport to Mr. Morton, the American consul in Salzburg. He has been very helpful. Emily's passport was returned in a plain brown business envelope addressed to Fred Stern, Rockville, Illinois.

"Fred, you didn't have to clear the dishes."

"Just a habit, Helen. I eat, I clear. I wash, I dry. I put back in the dish rack."

"Once in a while you could go out to dinner."

"It's easier at home."

If I Could Sleep . . .

Dining with the Rockville Journal. Obituaries and the TV schedule. Only features worth reading.

"You could go to the meal site at the Center."

"I go—once a year."

"Fred, you are not willing to help yourself."

Which means, Fred, how can I help you if you won't help yourself? That's what Helen wants. To improve my lifestyle. Absolutely American to seek improvement. Every day in every way...

"Fred, can I throw out the magazines? They are everywhere."

"I'll sort them out."

Sit and do your needle point, read Danielle Steel. Leave it to me to throw out The New Yorker, The Sunday Times, Granta . . .

"You know, Helen, there are some great short stories in The New Yorker."

"I don't read as much as I should."

"No one does."

"Your light was on half the night."

"I was reading Wallace Stegner."

The joyous advantages of aging. Fragmented sleep patterns, up in an hour, up and to the bathroom, read a short story, sleep for two hours, up and drink my 2 a.m. glass of red Zinfandel, sleep for two hours.

The New York Times slides onto the drive at 3 a.m. I can do the headlines, eat my Grapenuts and skimmilk and be back into bed by four.

"Fred, what time did you get up?"

"About six a.m."

"You could try to sleep a bit longer."

I try for you . . . Papa sang the hits of the '30s.

That's I cry for you, Papa.

When Emily was four she would sing the hymns from the Saturday service. Adon Olam asher malach.

Papa, did you teach Emmy?

No Fred, Emily retains the songs of the liturgy.

But Emily had her problems with statistics. We all have holes in our head.

I am an old, bent and tired man who will grin and throw back his shoulders when he greets the consolers.

"Fred, do I have to change my clothes? That is, for visitors."

Helen, in her simple grey woollen designer sack dress. Helen is wearing slippers, upholding the tradition for my sake.

Helen doesn't have to sit on a low stool. Emmy was only her niece. It's the father who sits on the low stool.

"No, Helen, you are fine as you are."

"Where are you going?"

"Where? Nowhere for the next three days. Just wandering around an empty house."

"Fred, I am here."

"It was good of you to come, Helen."

My brother Fred, a widower at sixty two, shuts himself up in an old house Papa built. Fred inherited the house that I should have gotten.

You got half a condo in Florida which was worth as much as the house in Oak Hills.

"Fred, go change your clothes. Look at yourself, you are a good looking man. Why do you neglect yourself so? Didn't you notice how filthy your sweatshirt is?"

"That's a shirt I use for the yard."

"No need to be filthy, Fred."

If I Could Sleep . . .

"It's just a couple of spots. I don't look at myself."

Fred, don't forget to zip up your fly. That's next.

"I'll change, don't worry, Helen. I'll go right up and change. Early supper tonight, Helen. We can expect the first callers about six."

Suntan trousers, white cotton buttondown shirt and sweatsocks, sandals. What a welldressed mourner wears for Shiva.

"Fred, it's cold in the house!"

"It gets cold when the sun goes down. I'll turn up the heat."

Chapter Four

I sit on a low stool wearing slippers. These are the traditions of the seven days of Shiva, the initial period of mourning during which the community will come to the Stern Home to console the bereaved. I, the bereaved, do not leave my house. I must speak first or there will be no conversation. I must talk, or endure talk, of Emily without excessive display of grief, for that too, is forbidden.

I will carry the grief, the loss, forever quietly and for eternity. For the next eleven months I will avoid my customary seat at the synagogue. Every day I will recite the mourner's Kaddish, the memorial prayer for the dead in praise of God. At the end of the year of mourning, and every year thereafter, I will sanctify Emily's memory by reciting the Kaddish on her Yahrtzeit—the anniversary of her death—and I will say Yizkor—the communal prayer in remembrance of the dead—on the designated Holy Days.

"Fred, you okay? You are so quiet."

"Just been thinking."

"You think too much, you pray too much. No wonder you haven't any time for yourself."

"That's possible, very possible."

"You ought to go out. Go for a little walk."

"The birds are eating my grass seed."

If I Could Sleep . . .

Helen is like Mama. Too often Mama reminded my father, Ben, you are not a clever man. What I always thought Mama meant was that Papa didn't protect himself, didn't spare himself, kept abusing his arthritic body, kept doing yardwork, kept going to his office. No wonder your father can't sleep at night. His legs ache and twitch and spasm. Papa should hire his yardwork done.

Then I am beholden to my yardman.

Ben, we are all beholden.

Then Mama would redirect her attack to an area where Dad was defenseless. Money.

Spend your money, Ben. Hire your yardwork. Your children will waste your money on luxuries. Anyway, they don't need your money.

Matty, you are right. I'll get some help.

That was Thursday. On Sunday Dad was in the yard raking last year's oakleaves from the evergreen ground cover, freeing the dried leaves from the entrails of the vinca border.

"What are you thinking about, Fred?"

"We'll have to repair the corn field. We can't delay the corn planting any longer."

"Sell off that six acres, Fred. Get rid of it."

"One day we'll have lots on that six acres."

"You're like Papa. Ten years, twelve years, fourteen years. You never give up. You should have sold when the city changed your zoning."

"I tried to get around it. It just went badly."

"George says you had a stupid lawyer."

"He was recommended to me."

"Dotty told me what happened. Dotty knew he didn't understand zoning the moment she spoke to him."

"He didn't do his homework. He never presented the case correctly. The funds were there waiting for me.

"Sure, Fred. You would have built housing for the elderly and made a fortune."

"We may do as well if we lay out lots for single family dwellings."

"Sure, next year. That's fourteen years later. Fred, you are not getting any younger."

Everything takes longer. I am slower. I wake up at six, but I can't get to the office until 9:30. Three hours. I read the paper, have breakfast, do my stretches, go to services. That's an hour and a half every morning for prayer and study. But, as written in the Ethics of the Fathers, if not now, when?

"What are you reading, Fred?"

"Crossing to Safety."

"Who wrote that?"

"Wallace Stegner."

"Danielle Steel is a better read."

Dad read veterinary journals. Mama read romantic Polish novels. Dotty read the contemporaries. Updike and Cheever, a lot of Roth and Malamud, always Singer and Bellow. Sinclair Lewis and Dos Passos too.

Younger then.

"Fred, can I turn on the weather station? It's raining again. Turn up the heat, Fred, I am cold."

Helen sits in her designer dress doing needlepoint. Sits in the corner armchair looking at the paintings that cover the livingroom wall, the prints Papa left me. Counting the days, only three more days of Shiva. But you'll have to wait until I am dead until you get the Matisse lithograph. I promised Black Eyes to you, Helen, but you'll have to wait. For my sister, Helen Gordon, the 1914 Matisse lithograph as a parting gift from her brother.

If I Could Sleep . . .

"Fred, do you have any idea of the value of Papa's art collection?"

Helen wants to be sure she got her fair share. Helen, you received exactly what Papa wanted you to have. Inheritance is not about equality. Everything was as Papa wished. Your brother Fred got more because Fred earned more, stayed in Rockville, paid the price.

"I'm hoping to get Sotheby's in for an appraisal."

"When, Fred?"

"I am hoping to, I am planning to, I'll try to."

"When was the last appraisal? Don't tell me, I know, eight years ago.

"I didn't get an appraisal when Dotty died."

"Doesn't your insurance company want an up to date appraisal?"

"I dropped the insurance."

"You saving your money? For what? A man in your position couldn't find the money to pay an insurance premium? Don't tell me that."

"It became troublesome. Forms, visits from the underwriters, do this, do that, add more alarms, change that."

"Fred, you never told me."

We have never had a loss, Mr. Wilcox. This is Rockville, not Chicago.

Mr. Stern, if you expect to buy insurance on your collection, you must add another motion alarm.

I understand.

I am afraid that you don't, Mr. Stern. You will not be insured unless you add that alarm.

That's my choice, Mr. Wilcox. I understand, Mr. Wilcox. You had a hard day's drive from Chicago. You have to make your recommendations to the underwriters.

What kind of business are you in, Mr. Stern, that you are willing to take risks? The underwriters demands are very minimal. I don't think going without insurance is the way to go.

Alex B. Stone

Let me tell you a story, Mr. Wilcox, about my father who always did the right thing, the safe thing. A man who was a friend to man and beast. My father saved on himself. You know what he enjoyed most? Sitting at home listening to modern music. Satie, Schoenberg. Every penny my father saved, he bought these American Modernist paintings. That, when no one in Rockville or New York cared about Dove and Demuth or Guy Pene du Bois. He sat home, read catalogs—there were no artbooks then, not like now. So Papa studied Sotheby catalogs. Papa bought the Demuth Tulips. That's the watercolor there. Look at the petals, lovely shade of the most thin, delicate purple wash I have ever seen. That watercolor came from the Demuth estate sale. Papa did without and bought what he loved and insured the paintings, the watercolors, the prints. But Papa did not insure his life adequately. My mother received only enough to live on. That is, until she sold some paintings.

But Mr. Stern! Isn't that all the more reason to insure the paintings?

Mr. Wilcox. I have adequate life insurance. The chance is very small that anything will happen to the paintings. On the other hand, the odds are in favor of me dying before my spouse.

"Fred, you are just like Papa."

"Helen, did you hear the owl last night?"

"No wonder you don't sleep."

"The owl woke me."

The wheels started turning. I got to thinking about Papa and Mama. Emily and Jack, too.

"You going to insure the collection when you get the appraisal?"

"I guess, if I can find a carrier that doesn't want me to turn my home into a bank vault."

"Have you started looking?"

"I called an agent in New York."

"Fred, can you remember when we were young and poor? I had

only one red cotton dress for school. Every evening Mama washed—and the little handkerchief that was pinned on my chest—washed and ironed and the next day I was all clean and starched."

"Die maydel mit dem royten kladel. Girl with Red Dress."

"Still speaking Yiddish?"

"Mamaloshen. What I learned at Mama's knee I don't forget. Your dress was a checked gingham with embroidered lace collar."

"I can't forget either, Fred. I just don't talk about it as much as you."

"We are all different."

"Still, I'm grateful I left Rockville."

"Are you still talking about being poor, Helen? That was fifty five years ago."

"I couldn't stand poverty."

"You got out."

"Though you didn't do so bad, Fred, right here in Rockville."

"It took me longer."

"What's so funny that you are laughing?"

"I was just thinking how hard each of us worked at making it, fulfilling the American Dream. Up from poverty. Mama was so pleased when you married money."

"Fred, when you talk like that I don't know what you are saying."

"I meant, Mama was pleased when you married George and became a Park Avenue Gordon. Papa missed you very much. It took him years to realize that you were grown and gone."

"We came home once a year."

"Yes, you did—until Rachel started school. What was the name of that private school Rachel went to?"

"St. Agatha's. Papa couldn't get it through his head that St. Agatha's was the best school for Rachel. We couldn't live in Manhattan and send Rachel to a public school. I am not a suburbanite, Fred. I enjoy living in the city. I know Papa wanted me to send Rachel to a Jewish day school. Whom would Rachel meet in a Jewish day school?"

Helen's route into society. Rachel at St Agatha's, the Episcopalian dayschool, where Helen, who hated poverty, would meet old Newyork money. Look at Helen today. She certainly found her own element. Helen's weekly Tuesday Art and Music in New York City Letter to her downhome brother in Rockville. I went to a private viewing of these wonderful neverexhibited paintings by Dubuffet, Rauchenberg, and Jim Dine. Then, just a few of us docents were invited for lunch. I was sitting next to the director of the Hirshhorn, Jim Demetrius. You may remember him, he was in Des Moines years and years ago. Next week I lecture on Afro American Art in the 'Fifties to a class of New Jersey retirees.

Helen can lecture on eighteenthcentury Czech porcelain, contemporary French crystal and Wiener Werkstätte furniture—and she knows the saleprice differentials between Paris, New York and Prague. Funny how life works. Rachel went to a Christian day school and married a Jewish boy. Edith and Edna went to Rockville's Hebrew school right through high school. Then they go down to Champaign because that's where the Jewish boys are and they both marry goyim!

Marriage a personal contract, Fred. Raising the children Jewish. Bill did convert.

"What did you say, Fred?"

"I didn't say."

"I thought I heard you."

"I said, I'll cut the grass on Sunday."

Chapter Five

"Fred, you should have remarried. Dotty has been gone eight years."

What Helen is saying is, Fred, you should have acquired a new wife. A new life. Spent your money to ease your days.

It's not the money, Helen, it's the effort. Getting a new wife is not like getting a new Lincoln. Choose from this year's colors. Darkblue with matching blueleather interior or contrast your interior with greyleather seats.

"You have the money, spend it. Your daughters don't need it"

Helen wants to know how much her brother has, how much he'll leave to her and her wonderful daughter and those two frenchprattling, hyperachieving grandchildren.

The farm isn't worth what it was six years ago. You have your eye on the art collection. You like those late Gustons, don't you?

I am leaving everything to Edith and Edna. They don't need it, but neither do your Francophile Episcopalian granddaughters. Helen, you won't get anything more from the artcollection than the 1914 Matisse print. That's all you get, Helen. Edith will use her inheritance to fund abortion clinics in Upper Volta, Mali, or some other dehydrated military dictatorship. Edna is the impatient one. She will ask for an advance on her inheritance so she can be Edna Stern Henricks, your Democratic Congresswoman from California.

Papa, if Feinstein and Boxer can be elected to the Senate, why shouldn't I run for Congress?

You are right, Edna. Emily is dead. You each get an extra 50% and you will have sufficient funds to run for Congress.

If I Could Sleep . . .

"Emily should have married and had children. You should have remarried, Fred."

Fred, you should. Fred, you shouldn't. Fred, we should spend more time with the girls.

You meant well, Dotty, but you didn't allow me my due. I didn't need much, just a few kind words now and then. That was good planning, Fred. Thank you, Fred.

My business successes took too long. By then the girls were gone, scattered. You educated three daughters, not one has ever put her arms around you and said Thank you, Dad, or I love you, Dad. Could be you weren't the father they wished for, but that was thirty years ago. Children don't forgive, don't forget.

Soon it will be too late. I'll be dead and my daughters will regret not spending more time with their father. It's always too late. It was too late for me. I never did realize how difficult my parents' lives were. Mama, what was it like for you during the War? Papa gone, no word from Papa's aunt or grandfather in Poland. Gone, all gone.

Edith and Edna will inherit the photographic history of the dead Sterns. From northern Poland to Rockville Hebrew Cemetery, Illinois, in sixtysix years.

"Helen, I told Edith and I told Edna last December—that was before Emily died—when we were in Florida, I want to die at home. Right here looking out at the oaks. Helen, if I can arrange a family plot would you like . . ."

"Fred, I have had enough of that kind of talk these last few days."

"I thought you should know how I felt."

"You told me when Dotty died. You don't have to worry, I didn't forget. That's the only way I would consider coming back to Rockville, to be buried in the family plot."

Every time Helen hears Rockville, there are Mama and Papa working so hard just to earn a living.

Later it got easier for them.

Sure. Papa didn't spend an extra penny until he was fifty, and Papa didn't pay off the home until he was sixtytwo.

46

Alex B. Stone

I found Mama's copy of Bellow's Sammler's Planet. Papa had written on the dedication page, May 30, 1970. For my dear wife. My first hedonistic act which I hope to continue.

Of course he didn't. Poor Papa, programed by the poverty experience. The immigrant experience.

Papa almost always made the wrong decisions.

Tried too hard to do the right thing. Thought it was his duty, his paternalistic duty, to be kind and generous to his one employee. Papa knew that Vince became violent when he drank. Papa knew, but Papa cared for Vince's wife, his daughter, so Papa didn't fire him. So, Papa got his head bashed in by an alcoholic employee. Papa, in his greystriped coveralls on his back, on the gurney in the emergency room of the Rockville hospital.

Fred, I can't see you.

Papa was fortunate he regained his vision, but after the Vince incident, every straight line that Papa looked at had a wave in it. What did Papa say when he came home? Thank God. It could have been worse. I could have had a permanent vision loss. The thought of not being able to read is what frightened me, Fred.

Fred, you are just like your father. Everyone takes advantage of you.

You are right, Dotty. Dotty, you don't have to yell at me. I hear you Dotty. I tried, Dotty, I just couldn't please you.

"Tell me, Fred, why didn't you remarry?"

"I sank into the routines of living alone."

Mothersday I go to the International Artfair in Chicago. Fathersday is with one of my dutiful daughters.

Emily, Edith, Edna, they knew whose turn it was to have dear old Dad. This year I will be with Edna in California. No. This year I am staying home. Edna was here for Emmy's funeral.

What is there to celebrate in being a father? The girls pass me around. They do the right thing for their widowed father. Flowers on my birthday. Once a year, one week of togetherness at the condo on Sanibel. We eat together, we read together, and once in a while Edith or Edna will say Papa, come for a walk with me. Just you and me. I want to talk to you. Just once talk to me before it's too late.

"It was easier not to remarry. I sort of slid into the pattern. And when I started to slide into it I never took the trouble to stop, to dig in my heels, to change direction."

"You don't look like you enjoy being alone all that much."

"There are times. It doesn't really matter, Helen. It will all be over for me soon enough."

"Don't get depressive on me"

"I'm not being depressive."

"You sound depressive."

"I'll try to be more up."

"Fred, what are you going to do when I leave? Go right back to where you were?"

Sundays I read the New York Times, write in my journal, write my three letters to my three daughters, each receives a personalized history of the week.

Two letters now.

Then there is the yardwork. Yesterday there was a grey squirrel looking for acorns in the driftwood pile I brought back from Sanibel. Pleased myself arranging it around the oak base. There on the lawn just four feet away was a rabbit watching the squirrel.

Not easy to grow grass under those oaks. I started reseeding last fall, did two reseedings this spring. Ford's Shady Mix does the best. I mix the grassseed into the ash from my burn pile, add an equal amount of peat and spread.

Dotty, I can't garden without a burn pile. What am I to do with the prunings from the Viburnum?

Fred, you are polluting the neighborhood.

Everyone burns, Dotty, not just me.

From you I expect better.

Helen watches me contemplating the lawn.

"Your lawn looks good, Fred."

"Thank you, Helen."

"Anything you want for supper?"

"Anything you like, the veal chops are fine."

The simpler the food the better. A lettuce tomato salad, some mozzarella cheese on black Balkan pumpernickel that I buy in Chicago. It's the bread makes the meal. For lunch I eat a lettuce salad and matzo. Matzo, the bread of affliction. For we were slaves in Egypt and we fled in haste.

"You want dessert?"

"Whatever you like, Helen."

"You are no help."

"I eat everything."

"No you don't. You didn't eat my stir fry."

Complaining about food is bad manners, Fred. Yes, Mama. Complaining is commentary on life, Mama.

"Whatever you like, Helen, is fine with me."

"When did you say most of the callers will come to pay their condolences?"

"About seven, seven thirty. Won't anyone stay later than nine thirty."

"It's a shame you never learned to cook, Fred. George is doing all our cookouts."

George, in his whitestarched chefspouf, George embroidered in red cursive on his apron, George, an asbestos mitt in his left hand, a twoprong turningfork in his right. Rare? Medium? How do you like your steaks? Steaks to order on blissful summer Sunday afternoons with Helen and George Gordon on the lawn of their tastefully, authentically restored, 18th century Dutch colonial cottage overlooking the Hudson.

"The veal chops good?"

"I ate two."

"You could have done better than marry Dotty Harris."

"Not that again, Helen. That was almost fifty years ago."

"I can't forget."

Forget, forgive, God's gift of time. You can't forget, I can't remember.

Fred, why remember? One lifetime, one chance. You had good years, you had not so good years. You win, you lose, average earnings is all that anyone gets. Some do good when they are young, I did better when I became older. At least it was more peaceful.

"Dotty had the most awful temper."

"Don't start in, Helen, with all the Harrises had bad tempers. Jack was as fine a young man as ever lived. Kind, generous, giving."

"So he died when he was twenty five."

"You don't have to remind me, Helen. It was twenty three years this February.

"Dotty was a very charitable human being."

"Not to you, Fred."

"Dotty had her opinions."

"Opinions, huh! Dotty was always right. I heard her. You didn't think I knew but I heard her screaming at you."

"Dotty didn't think I heard her unless she yelled. Dotty has been dead for eight years. Let her be, Helen."

"Dotty didn't appreciate you."

It's true Dotty didn't approve of my writing. You know why, Fred. Because, if you had made it, if you had been successfully published, she would have been wrong about your stories. You don't write stories, Fred, you write little sketches. Dotty didn't like to be wrong. You are right, Dotty. Whatever you wish, Dotty.

"I'll clear."

"You sit, Fred."

"I always clear."

"For Dotty you cleared. Men with feminist wives clear, cook, diaper the children."

"I bathed the girls."

I can't remember Emily as a baby. At five she was a cowboy, her cowboyhat held in place with a leather thong under her chin. At her little hips, two toy pearlhandled pistols in tooled leather holsters. Papa went downtown to Walgreen's with Emily in his charge. Bang! she pointed the pistol at Ken the store manager. Bang! he shot back at her. Ken called when he read the obituary.

"What are you thinking about, Fred? You look very pensive."

"I have to find the slides."

"What slides, Fred? What are you talking about?"

Emily's first day at school. I took more than thirty photos that day. Emily and Dotty hand in hand. I walked behind and ahead, right on Fifth Avenue to McKinley School, up the steps to the kindergarten. I can't remember what Emily was wearing.

Dotty was only twentyeight, bestlooking woman in Rockville. Fred, that was thirtyseven years ago.

Yesterday, just yesterday.

When Helen leaves, I'll look for the slides. I'll sort the slides. The Sterns in Colorado. Dotty and Fred in Mexico. Dotty and Fred in Israel. I'll dump them all on the table, label them, let Edna or Edith decide what to do with the Sterns on bluefaded 35mm Kodacolor.

Let them throw them out. That's what children are for. You save fortyyearold slides, thirtyyearold hats, they throw them out.

"Fred, you are a pack rat. Look at the top shelves of your hall closet! There are six hats."

A grey cowboy model, never worn. A Tyrolean hat with a red feather. That's the hat the Stanford marching band wore. Two narrowbrim felt dresshats, one brown, one grey, a black cap with earmuffs. Emily brought that one back from Italy for me the first time she went skiing in Europe. There. The Italian maker's crest on the lining.

"Fred, this is no life for you. Nobody can help you if you won't help yourself."

The evenings are peaceful. Monday through Fridays I watch McNeal Lehrer. Tuesdays I read, Wednesdays I read, Thursdays I watch Mystery, Fridays I do Week In Review. Saturdays I rest, Sundays I garden or go to an afternoon movie or to the Chamber Music Concert. Then, it's Monday again.

"What do you want me to do, chase widows?"

"Go out to dinner on Saturday night, go dancing at the Coliseum. You don't have to get so upset with me, it's for your own good, Fred."

I know whatisgoodforyou. The most detestable phrase in the English language. Your life would have been different if you had listened to me. Different is not better, Dotty. At least less stressful without all your stupid business deals.

Dotty was right. Into a deal was easy. Out was difficult to impossible. Business, always business, got in the way of your family life, got into the way when you should have been with the children. The girls should forgive and forget and understand too.

"Fred, you nodded off. You fell asleep while I was talking to you."

Can't sleep at night. Fall asleep well enough, but then up at 1, drink a glass of wine, sleep till 2, drink a glass of milk, sleep until 5:30. Wake up tired, go to sleep tired. It's a disease syndrome, fragmented sleep patterns. Take your medicine. Mayo's has changed your prescription three times. I can't take those pills. It makes me drugstupid. Is that better than being stupid tired?

Fell asleep on the Interstate while driving back from Chicago. I was fortunate, woke up when the front wheels hit the shoulder. We all live with miracles, that's what Papa said. It's not your turn to die yet, Fred.

"I don't sleep well."

"You don't take your pills. Edith told me."

Chapter Six

"Was that the door?"

"It's the side door, Helen."

"I'll get it. You sit there. I'm sure it's someone to see you."

Helen turns at the threshold between the sitting room and the kitchen, murmurs, "Looks like you have a lady caller, Fred. A very goodlooking lady."

"You remember Mary Belkin, don't you, Helen? Mary married Manny Gross. You remember?"

"Don't get up, Fred, I'll take the rocker. My folks owned Belkin Tailors and Cleaners on Fourth Avenue near the Courthouse."

Mary is not yet fifty. Look at her. Buys grandma clothes in K Mart. Least she could do is buy those horrid rayon prints large enough to disguise her pupik and her tuchiss. Her makeup is twenty years ago. Lips too red. Her scent arrives before her and will linger after. But that's Rockville!

"Mary's mother always asked about you. You remember Mary's mother?"

Short and squat, like Mary, with the yellow tape measure around her neck and that perpetual toplease blueeyed smile smiling from behind the counter while she took in the cleaning. You hear Jake, what Miss Stern wants? Jake nods, bends back to his Singer foottreadle sewingmachine. Mary's mother's name was Bella. There were three kewpiedoll Belkin girls.

"Mary is Mrs. Gross now. Mary, you remember my sister Helen Gordon? Mary is our house manager at the synagogue."

"Whenever you came home for the holidays my mother may she rest in peace pointed you out to me. She said, Mary, the Stern girl is wearing a Clair McCardell designer dress. Look at those lines, so simple, so elegant. When you go by her, look at the material. See how it drapes, how the front falls. Those days, Mrs. Gordon, nobody in Rockville but you wore designer clothes."

"You didn't go into fashion?"

"I studied design, got married."

"Mary is married to Manny Gross—you remember, Comfy Mattress Company?"

"Must have been after my time."

"You are right, Mrs. Gordon. It was about thirty years ago that Manny and his dad came here from Chicago."

"Mary is doing a great job for the synagogue."

"Sometimes not so great. What we need we don't have. We don't have a caterer that can cook for more than twenty or thirty."

"Some of the folks have been bringing in caterers from Chicago. They come with everything from napkins to cleanup."

"I want to forget Joe Kessler's wedding. Joe invited one hundred and forty."

"The Kesslers are an older couple, Helen. You wouldn't know them. I was there. Everybody took it very well."

"Thank God."

"What happened?"

"What didn't? I'm trying to forget."

"Go ahead, tell Helen."

"The cook took the skin off the broilers before she put them in the oven and that's the way the chicken quarters were placed on the plate—not even with a little paprika to add color. The chicken came out clammy white, the string beans were from cans and then the cook burned one pan of the kugel so that she was short about forty pieces of kugel for those who were served last. Fred, you were one of the lucky ones. You didn't get any kugel."

At least I was invited to the Kessler wedding. That's more than my only sister Helen did when her Rachel married Guy Kahn in the study of the Grand Rabbi of Paris. Sorry, Fred, just a few of Rachel's friends from the embassy. A small private wedding. I do hope you and Dotty understand. We would love to have you come to Paris for the afterwedding reception. That will be in Rachel's new apartment. George and I do hope you can come. I am sorry I can't invite you, but you know how children are. Rachel and Guy wanted a very quiet affair. No big todo. After all, they have been living together. I am sure you knew that.

I am Rachel's only uncle. Your only brother. Dotty and I had already bought our airline tickets. We couldn't imagine not being invited. That, my boy, was fifteen years ago. Helen wouldn't reveal her Rockville relatives then, and don't be stupid, she wouldn't show you off now.

"Everything went wrong at the Kessler wedding. The wedding cake was eggless white layer cake. A layer of strawberry ooze and another layer of white cake. When the cook cut the cake, the cake crumbled into mush—came all apart. She was not daunted. She lifted the red sticky goo with her fingers onto the plate, smeared a dollop of strawberry sauce at one end of this delight and sent it out to the hundred and forty guests!"

"No one said a word."

"Not till the next day."

"I ate it."

"I don't know how you could, Fred, but then you were sitting in the back. You didn't see her fingers in the cake."

Nothing changes in Rockville. First they talk about the synagogue. Next she will tell us who is sick.

"How is Abe Frankel doing?"

"Thank God, Fred. Abe is still alive."

"Abe had an aneurysm repaired. Poor Abe. One surgery and two repairs in three weeks. It's a miracle he is still with us.

"If there is anything you need, Fred, you know we have frozen kosher meals. I'll bring them over myself."

"I'm doing all right."

"It's not easy to lose a wife and then a daughter. Thank God for Edith and Edna."

"They had to get home to their families."

"I heard they left."

"They call every day. Helen stayed and that does help."

"Everyone has been asking about you, Fred."

"Thank you for coming, Mary."

"Mrs. Gordon, you didn't have to get up, but, tell me. What happens with Fred after you go back? I am so worried about Fred living here all alone.

"I am, too, but you know Fred . . ."

"Fred, you used to hang around one of the Belkin girls, didn't you? That first summer you came home from college. The tall one, the one who went to the University of Illinois. What ever became of her?"

"That was Norma; she is in Atlanta. She teaches theoretical math at Emory. I wasn't exactly hanging around, Helen. I was selling Fuller Brushes store to store and door to door. Jake Belkin was kind enough to let me keep my stock of brooms in his back room."

In the corner by the Hoffman pressingmachine.

Alex B. Stone

Fred, you are going to be a big success.

Thanks, Jake.

I meant it, Fred.

That summer I made enough selling brushes to pay my way for another year at Champaign.

No state college for Helen Stern.

Judge to bankrobber: Why do you keep robbing banks? That's where the money is. University of Chicago. That's where the money was. George Gordon, University of Chicago and Harvard Law School, has joined his father in the practice of law at Jenkins, Gordon and McKee, 11 Wall Street, New York City.

"That little cleaning establishment made the Belkins a good living. Sent three girls through college."

The older Belkins died broke. The minute Bella left the store Frankie the bookie parked his purple Cadillac in the alley in back. Jake gambled away fifteen dollars a day on the horses, on the numbers. That was their fortune. I never said a word, not to a soul.

Made forty dollars a week selling brushes and that was more than a man earned working in the factories.

Fifteen dollars then was like ninety today. Maybe more like one hundredfifty. That, Fred, was 1940. Fiftythree years ago.

Mary at services every Saturday. Her father never came to Shul. Jake was an unrepentant nonbeliever. Show me, college boy, show me where is God. In Poland where the Germans are killing Jews? I read it in the Forward. Read it for yourself.

I can't read Yiddish.

Fred, you are going to make a lot of money.

How do you know, Jake?

I know.

Tell me.

You're the next generation. You understand America. You are going to college. Me, I went to work at twelve.

If I Could Sleep . . .

Jake Belkin never went to the synagogue. Jake didn't believe in God. Now his daughter is the backbone of the sisterhood.

"You believe in God, Fred?"

Fiftythree years ago Jake asked me the same question, and now Helen.

"I don't have the courage not to believe in God. I am not a brave man."

"You were in two wars."

"That had nothing to do with courage."

"You volunteered."

"That's duty, that's not bravery."

It takes more courage to believe in nothing than I could ever find in myself. I need God to help me through the days and nights.

"At least you and I can talk about God. Papa was no help. Papa always talked around everything."

"We are all different. Don't go blaming Papa for your problems between you and God."

"How can you believe, Fred?"

"I can't be left without hope. God is my hope. Some believe, some don't. Sometimes I believe more, sometimes I believe less."

"But you believe."

"That's all I have left."

"Fred, your eyes are shutting. Go lie down."

"I can sleep in the chair."

"I'm making myself some Earl Grey. You want some tea?"

"No thanks."

"I'll bring it to you. You won't have to get up."

"That's okay, Helen. I need to move around a little."

I'll have the outside of the house painted the same color, then I'll have the gutters replaced. Dotty chose cactus tan thirtyfive years ago. Earthtones were all the fashion then. Dotty, if you like cactus, I like cactus. Painting contractors are no help, they just want to please. Yes,

Alex B. Stone

Mr. Stern. That's fine, Mr. Stern.

The Morandi drawing has to be reframed with UV glass. Might just as well redo the Bellows at the same time—oval drawing by George Bellows that hangs to the right of the kitchensink where Dotty could see it. The mat on the Klimt should be changed to acidfree.

"You making lists again, Fred? Get some rest. You need to rest more, then maybe you wouldn't be so tired."

"You are right, Helen."

Dotty was always right. Mama was always right.

Dotty was for the simple life, take a job, save, get a fivepercent raise a year. Take twoweeks vacation, go visit the folks. You could teach at a small college. Every summer we could have a couple of months for ourselves to spend with the girls. A Sabbatical. Think of it, Fred. Every seventh year free.

Fred, why do you have to become a builder, developer? Who needs it?

Somebody has to do it.

Let someone else do it, Fred. Take the offer from the University of North Carolina.

I can't leave Mom and Dad.

Can't leave what we have in Rockville? Nothing but stress! First you fight for zoning, then you fight for financing, then you fight with the mortgage bankers. Everyone steals from you.

I got the job done. I built the first rentals for families with children.

What did that do for you, Fred?

Onehundredandsixty families have a decent place to live.

And you ended up with confrontations with the IRS. That took eight years of your life to settle. Don't talk to me about the money you made. It was nothing. Nothing for what it took from you in health. You are not all that well, Fred. You are being crippled by your arthritis.

Life has it's price. I fooled the doctors for almost thirty years.

If I Could Sleep . . .

When I came home from the Army—Go home, Captain Stern. In six months you'll be in a wheelchair. I did it myself, Dotty. Exercise, swimming, massage, whirlpool. I have only been hospitalized four times in forty years.

You are losing the fight, Fred. Your arthritis is gaining on you, Fred. Look at your wrists. How's your back, Fred?

Hurts. It always hurts.

The more stress, the worse your arthritis gets.

Dotty, I should have taken that job in North Carolina.

"Fred, it's your office. Somebody by the name of Ed. I told him you were resting but he said it was important."

"I should get up anyway."

"Fred, it's Pete again. The police have him. Same damn stupid thing again. He broke into the warehouse, kicked in five or six doors. Claims he can't remember a thing. Why would he kick in doors he has keys to? I spoke to the State's Attorney before I called you. He'll try to get Pete back on one of the alcohol rehab programs. I am sorry to bother you, Fred. I didn't want to tell you but I would say there is at least a thousand dollars damage to the doors."

"What did the State's Attorney say?"

"Keep a record of the cost of the repairs, but what do I do with Pete?"

"When is the hearing?"

"Next Tuesday."

"I don't know anymore, Ed."

"I know what I would do! Fire him, is what I would do."

"He has a wife and daughter."

"He is a stinking alcoholic. Willy is afraid of him when he gets violent."

"He has never put a hand on anyone."

"Not yet!"

"Okay, I'll tend to it next Tuesday when I come back."

"Fred, you want me to pay him off? I would make him pay for the damages is what I would do."

"Pay him. No sense punishing him now. He doesn't understand."

"Fred, this is the second time."

"We'll reach a decision when I come back. Everything else okay?"

"Fine, Fred. Just fine."

"Thanks, Ed."

"Can't they leave you alone? Fred, you lost a daughter and your office calls you."

"Ed means well. He needed my input to reach a decision."

To be in business today, you have to be Solomon. I never had a rabbi, a teacher, a role model. That's what they call a mentor now. I suffered and learned slowly, painfully. I was used, abused, stolen from and you still made it, Fred. Not big, maybe. Could have done better in North Carolina. I'd be retired by now, living on a pension, live anywhere I wished. Could do that now. Why don't you, Fred? Do something for yourself before it's too late.

"Helen, I put it off until Tuesday."

"Put what off?"

"What to do with Pete. Troubles, Helen. All God's children got troubles, frustrations. Pete can't handle his, so he gets drunk kicks in doors."

"In the middle of the afternoon?"

"Such is life in the bluecollar fast lane. A couple of boilermakers on your lunch hour, come back to your job, kick in the doors and you get a week's vacation with pay."

"You should have remarried, Fred. You should have married a woman that could help you in the business, like Dotty did."

"You are right, Helen."

Chapter Seven

"I'll get the door, Fred."

"I'll get it, Helen."

"Rabbi Kaplan, my sister Helen."

"We met at the funeral."

"May we meet only on happy occasions. And Fred, may you be comforted with all the mourners of Israel."

"Tea, Rabbi?"

"Please. With a little artificial sweetener and lemon. You have lemon. I know you have lemon. I suppose you know what your brother did two years ago? Two weeks in a row at the Friday night Kiddush—we serve cookies and tea after Friday night services—there was no lemon, don't ask me why. So the next Monday I get from your brother a check for fifty dollars from the Stern Foundation to provide lemons for our congregation. Fred had an investment schedule all worked out. Fifty dollars invested at five percent a year would yield two dollars and fifty cents to provide our congregation with lemons in perpetuum. That's how I know you have lemons!"

"I am sorry, Rabbi, I didn't go shopping. There is some lemon juice in the refrigerator."

"That will be fine.

"You know, your brother is something of a legend in our

community."

On the Herman Miller table the Dansk teaset that Dotty bought so well at the outlet. Helen in the rocker, knitting and nodding approval to the Rabbi.

"The death of a child, that is unnatural, that is out of the natural order. The children are supposed to bury the parents, not the parents the children. Such a loss, such a talented young woman. So accomplished. What can I say to comfort you?"

Say? No matter what you say there are no answers. No answers.

"What can anyone say, Rabbi?"

"Psalm twenty three of David says all that can be said. The Lord is my shepherd, I shall not want. He makes me lie down in green pastures, he leads me beside still waters. He restores my soul. He leads me on paths of justice for the sake of His Name. Even if I shall walk through the valley of the shadow of death . . . You'll be coming back to the morning Minyan?"

"I'll be there Monday."

"When is your sister leaving?"

"Sunday afternoon."

"I have been here a week. I came down as soon as I heard.

"I called Helen as I got the news . . . "

"Fred, I hope you will come back to the Talmud study."

"Why wouldn't I?"

"The sooner the better. You've passed through a terrible ordeal."

The Babylonian Rabbis taught their communities a harsh lesson. The death of a child is punishment for the sins of the prior generations, the sins of the fathers. Thank God that today the survivors are not blamed for their own sorrow, responsible for their loss. Dead is dead, gone is gone.

Dotty is gone. Emily is gone. Whom to blame? No one to blame. There is still so much in our lives to be thankful for. Listen to Helen. Next week when the Rabbi will raise you from your mourning you will praise God in the Kaddish that you will recite every day for eleven months.

"Tell me, Fred, how are you feeling? Physically, I mean."

"I'll do better when I get back to swimming."

"You are not moving so well, Fred."

"Add a little old age to arthritis . . ."

"My joints give me a twinge too now and then. The old barometer, you know. . ."

"Your barometer is still young, Rabbi Kaplan."

When was I ever young? Once I was young, but not for long. Fred, no one is interested in your life stories.

"You have a beautiful yard, Fred. You care for it well."

By the chainlink fence, the house for purple martins—house with the blue roof that never housed martins—only barnsparrows. Propped twelve feet up by a telescoping white enamel pole. As I was erecting the house, the shaft collapsed, the house hit me on the head. Left a purple bruise. A portent?

Lucky, always lucky. Worldwar II, Korea, two headon crashes. Not a scratch, not a fracture! Because of prayer. Others pray . . . next door, Katy prays to her Catholic God to heal her daughter Alice's arthritis. At age twentyfive Alice has had two hip replacements.

"Such a beautiful tea service, Mrs. Gordon."

Dansk is the everyday company service. When Dotty and I ate alone, Dotty used the British Victorian pewter pot with the rattan handle. For her infrequent tea parties Dotty chose the French silver set which she hated to polish. The silver is in the closet. Silver trays, silver icecream spoons, silver flatware service for twelve.

It took Dotty an age until she bought anything. Only time she reached a quick decision was when Emily chose her crystal pattern. I'll take a dozen for ourselves, Fred and a dozen for each of the girls and when I go the girls can fill in their sets with my crystal.

Dotty is gone, the crystal is in the closet waiting—waiting for me to go, waiting for Edith and Edna to fill in their crystal.

"My sister in law had good taste, Rabbi."

"I should go now. I mustn't tire you out, Fred. Try to get some rest."

"Thank you for coming, Rabbi."

"I look forward to seeing you at Shabbat services. Remember: it is not permitted to grieve on the Shabbat!

"Good bye, Mrs. Gordon. Don't get up, Fred."

"I was getting up anyway . . . keeps me limber."

"Fred gets up every hour on the hour."

"I thought he would have more callers," I overhear Helen complain at the front door.

"Helen, I'm going out for just a second."

"Put on a coat."

The spring rains have turned the sod into a mud molerun. The winterkilled oaklimbs, the debris of each windstorm wait to be collected, to be put on the burn pile, to become ash to be spread on the lawn in spring reseeding. Ashes to ashes, dust to dust. Jews don't say that, Fred. That's only on the latenight horror movies. Dank dark foggedin British graveyards overhung by Gothic church and Oxford accents, the priest, the sexton lantern in hand beside him, recites the burial liturgy. Dustodust.

"Fred, is that a Mercedes the Rabbi is driving?"

I have nineteen oaks, onehundredsixtyyearold oaks on a quarter of an acre. The oaks were here before we built our home among them. They will be here after you are gone, Fred. I'll have the oaks topped off. This will add hours of afternoon sunlight to brighten the kitchen and dining room. It has been ten, twelve years since the oaks were last thinned. Call the tree service on Tuesday.

Fred, you have more important things to do than worry about your oaks.

Dotty found the lot in Oak Hills when I was in Korea. A quiet neighborhood culdesac with respectable homes neither ostentatious nor pretentious where the neighbors nod and stop to visit for a second or two. The Stern home, around the corner from the synagogue, a board and batten twostorey fourbedroom, painted in the earthtones of the '60s. In Rockville there is really no such thing as a Jewish neighborhood. The neighbors to the west are Jewish, and down and across the street there is another Jewish family. The nextdoor neighbors are the only ones I will visit without a telephone call. Our girls are gone, their children are gone. I wait for the rechildrening of Oak Hills.

What about the Gibsons? The Gibsons have children.

The Gibsons an Afroamerican family with three small children live across the street in the brick colonial with the central stair. The Browns—that's the third on the left—have sold and will be moving to Arkansas. That will bring bouncing basketballs and coughing motorcycles.

In Rockville, where the Mississippi flows from east to west, where the first railroadbridge crossed the mighty Mississippi, there is an island in the river where the Confederate States prisoners dead from smallpox and typhoid are buried in square rows.

In the downtown, where once there were two operahouses, now there are none. One became the movietheatre, became the pornohouse, today stands empty with For Sale on the marquee. The other one died earlier with vaudeville. When the modestly priced downtown hotel for traveling salesmen was torn down, it went with it, to be replaced by a glassfront, threestorey modern officebuilding with a leaking roof.

"Fred?"

"I'll be right in."

"It's cold out there."

The lilac is gnarled, aged, only extreme pruning will save it. Cut out the driedout, the dead. Next year new branches will seek the spring's thin sun.

"Would you like some lilacs, Helen? I'll cut them for you."

"Fred, it's dark out there. Come in. What were you doing out there?"

"Just looking. Thinking what has to be done."

"Fine supper, Helen. Thank you."

"Fred, you could at least learn to use your grill. I saw the grill outside the gazebo. Why don't you use it?"

Why don't I use the grill? Why don't I buy a CD player? Why don't I use the espresso machine? Why don't I? Why don't I use the vegetable steamer Edna bought? Why . . . ?

"I'll tell you why. It's easier for me not to."

"Fred, I did the laundry."

"Okay, I'll put on a clean shirt."

According to the tradition, I should sit the entire Shiva week in the same shirt. Dirty unwashed unshaven and uncombed, my appearance overcome by grief.

Alex B. Stone

I hope Helen doesn't start in with Fred when are you going to start living? Last night's coming attraction, previews of the next three days, followed by the main feature, What Did You Do With All The Money You Made?

I told you I set the money aside to pay my estate taxes.

Rockville is not Manhattan but neither is it a village. We are the sixtythird largest metropolitan area in the entire USA, and I own more than a bit of downtown. Is that a good reason for me to stay here? I don't know, Helen. I don't know.

What is living in Rockville doing for you, Fred?

Keeps me busy, Helen. Keeps me frustrated, keeps me alert, keeps me full of hope. Keeps me in despair when I remember that the bad times have been here for so long. Thirteen, fourteen years since the factories closed. As soon as I rent up downtown I sell out. I don't want to quit just yet. I think next year or the year after things will turn around.

You don't need the money, Fred.

Pride, Helen. Pride in my vision of tomorrow. I bought an officebuilding when it was all but empty.

It has remained all but empty. You gave it twelve good years of constant effort so quit! Walk away! Financial success is the American measurement. Lifestyle is more important, Fred.

"Fred, you still playing tennis with Sherman Karp?"

"Every second Sunday."

Sherman's still beating you. That's because of my arthritis. You envy Sherman? Sherman has his sons in the business. Sherman has warehouses in Omaha and Fort Worth. Sherman can't quit either. Sherman has a fiftyyearold son and a fortyfiveyearold soninlaw waiting for him to stroke out.

Envious, vindicative I am not. You understand, Helen? Winning is better than losing. It's the American way. One thing I don't do is waste the present planning for revenge, vendettas against those who have beaten me. I will get rid of Belsky, though. Better yet, I'll get more than even. But I can wait. Four years, four months, Belsky's lease is up. Then he pays uptodate or else. Else what? No lease renewal? Fred, you'll be seventysix years old. I'll outlive that Belsky sonofabitch!

"Fred, do you want a sleeping pill?"

"No."

"You wander around all night."

"The wind is shifting to southwest. That will cut the humidity. The temperature will be falling."

Fred, you sniff the wind like an old coonhound on a night trail. Go inside, get your weather report on TV like the rest of the world. Maybe if you'd stuff those Solari wind chimes you would sleep better.

I no longer notice the chimes. Dotty loved their belltones.

"You sure you don't want a pill, Fred?"

"Only time I took pills was when I was in the hospital."

"You never told me you were hospitalized."

"What's to tell?"

"What happened?"

"I had a nerve loss to my left leg."

"Fred, if you had a wife . . . "

"I know. I could have spent my two weeks flat on my back at home in my own bed, taken care of by a kind doting loving caring young strong wife."

"Don't get sarcastic on me, Fred."

"No one enjoys taking care of a partially paralyzed old man. By the time I got to the hospital I was so bad I had to pee while I was flat on my back."

"Fred, don't get vulgar."

"That's not vulgar, Helen, that's sciatica!"

"That is painful!"

"Pain passes."

Alex B. Stone

"Why didn't you tell me?"

"So I told you. What would you do? Come to Rockville and nurse me? I'm sorry, Helen, I didn't mean for you to cry . . ."

"Did you at least tell your daughters?"

"I told them. I called them from the hospital, told each one I was doing fine."

Emily sent flowers. Chrysanthemums. I replanted them. Edith sent me a Paddington Bear to keep me company and Edna sent a donation to the synagogue. That was after I had been home for a week.

"I'm going to bed, Fred."

"I'll put out the lights."

"Fred, don't forget to put on the alarm."

"Nobody will rob us."

"Aren't you afraid living alone?"

"Good night, Helen."

"Fred, you could try just half a pill."

"Not tonight. I'll read for a while."

"Read in bed, Fred, it will make you sleepy."

"I'll try, Helen."

In The New Yorker a beautifully crafted shortstory by Alice Munro. An aging dejected dowdy deserted wife follows her middleaged husband and his young 28yearold love to Australia. The wife rents an apartment of a recently deceased woman, writes a series of letters to her husband which she signs with the name of the recently departed. As soon as the husband realizes that it is his wife that he is corresponding with, he confronts her. The jilted wife immediately leaves Australia, returns to her waiting life. Surely, the husband will follow her.

At 4 I look through the kitchen window at the Gibson colonial. The oak leaves obscure and obstruct the streetlight. The drive is dark but not as dark as the street in the 1954 Magritte painting Empire of Light.

If I Could Sleep . . .

At 5 I sleep. I awake at 6 too tired to get up, doze until 6:30, struggle out of bed at 7 to find Helen in the dining room hunched over the New York Times crossword in my Pierre Cardin bathrobe.

"Gets harder every day. It's already Thursday and I don't have half of the puzzle solved."

"There is a nine hundred number you are supposed to call and pay seventy five cents or ninety cents for each word. That's why the puzzle is so difficult, so that you pay to win."

"You ever do the puzzle, Fred?"

"Never. Waste of time."

"You never change. You, my brother, are very predictable. I cut your orange into squares."

"Thanks, Helen. You want a quarter section of orange?"

"Leave it, I'll eat it later. Your Grape Nuts are ready. Fred, do you ever eat anything but Grape Nuts?"

"Not as long as there is a dollar coupon in the Sunday paper."

Fred Stern: a man with all the American virtues extolled by Poor Richard. Who collects soap from the Holiday Inn. Uses his morning papernapkin for an afternoon handkerchief, never buys two of anything when one will do. A man who finds little joy in spending.

"What are you mumbling, Fred?"

"I said it's like in the Psalms: The dread dark of the night is dispersed by the morning's light.

"Today will be better for you, Fred."

"I hope."

"Did you sleep?"

"Would have if I could have."

Chapter Eight

"Fred, I finally figured out what is wrong with you."

"Don't tell me."

"Let me finish, let me talk. You never let Dotty talk, you don't let me talk."

"Okay, tell me."

"You worry too much about dying, so you end up praying too much."

"So?"

"I don't think it's healthy to be prayer dependent."

"You sound like Mama talking about sex."

"Fred! I mean you should get more diversion into your life. More outside interests."

"I function."

"You could be happier."

The new American dream. Everyone has to be happy. Each generation has its dream. My generation wanted to free Europe from Hitler. I wanted to save what Jews were left alive so I was pleased to bomb Germany. Nice clean work. Nothing personal, just dropping fivehundredpound bombs to destroy Germany's industrial and military assets.

Those factories had people working in them. Most weren't even

German. Later we learned they were slave labor; French, Dutch, Poles, gathered from all over Europe.

"You think too much."

I'm getting better. I didn't think too much about what I did in 1944 until the war started in Bosnia. The same killing, again justified by a philosophy. The Germans were going to cleanse Europe of Jews. Today, the Serbs are cleansing Muslims, the Muslims are cleansing Serbs. The Croats are cleansing Serbs, the Croats are cleansing Muslims. That's when I think of our bomber crew. Especially the ones that died.

Our bomber wing was the lucky one. We arrived in England in 1944 when the going was easy, when the German airforce was no longer a great threat. We did thirty daytime bomberruns over Germany without a loss. We were counting the days to get home on rotation before we were to be repositioned against the Japanese.

It was a Friday, my lastchance weekend to go to London to buy gifts for Mama and Papa. We came in high, bounced, bounced again. I could smell the stink of the burning gasoline. I jumped out. Why Billy Kahn, our tail gunner, couldn't get free in time I don't know. By the time the firefighting crew got to him, he was dead amidships from smoke inhalation. Staff Sgt. Billy Kahn, nineteen, the Brooklyn bantamweight, Eighth Airforce Boxing Champion. Billy sent home a picture of himself getting his trophy.

I'm in the cockpit, so I survive. Billy is aft, so he dies.

Still, if only I . . . .

First time I met Billy, you know what he said? Lieutenant Stern, I never met a Jew from anyplace but New York. You really from Rockville, Illinois?

On the way home I was in New York. Said to myself, Fred, you owe it to Billy, go see his parents. Tell them their son had a proper Jewish burial in the 8th Airforce Cemetery. There is a star of David over his grave. After the war maybe you could visit England. The cemetery is very close to Cambridge . . .

Lieutenant Stern, you should have no trouble finding Blake Avenue. Where the Seventh Avenue IRT line ends at a stop called Van Sicklen. When you come down the stairs, turn right for two blocks, then turn right for three blocks. One of us is almost always home, this afternoon is fine . . .

I found the fourstorey tan brick apartmenthouse on a treeless Brooklyn street. In the entry hall the paintedon oak wainscoting was scarred to the plaster. The hexagonal ceramic floortile with it's blue border was dulled by thirty years of applied wax. The worn slate treads, the splintered handrails, the lingering odor of Pinesol that did not bring the forest freshness to the justwashed landings, all spelled ghetto poverty that I had only read about in Sholem Aleichem's stories.

C4 Kahn was the thirdfloor front. Two bedrooms, a kitchen, a livingroom. Mrs. Kahn in her best skirt, whitesilk blouse, with a smile both tired and old. She couldn't have been more than fortyfive, but then I was only twentytwo.

"Come in . . . come in."

Mrs. Kahn led me to the green mohair sofa. She drew up a folding chair, sat opposite me and talked, talked. She did not succeed in making me feel at ease.

Lieutenant Stern, Velvel wrote about you. Velvel was a very good son. He wrote every week, just a few words in Yiddish to his father and to me in English. He told me all about you. Your parents should be very proud of you—you an officer.

I was in the college training program.

A collegeboy who won't eat pork. Your parents should be proud to have such a son.

Your son died so young. I am so sorry.

To us our son will always be nineteen.

I nodded.

If I Could Sleep . . .

You'll stay, you'll eat supper with us? My husband Herbie will be home soon.

So I who had come to console the parents on the death of their only son, sat and ate boiled chicken and boiled carrots and spongecake and heard from the bereaved parents only praise for America.

In Poland I never saw a Jewish officer. In Poland who ever heard of a Jew going to college? You know what? My Velvel wanted to be a doctor for children, for poor children. My Velvel could have been a doctor—and me a presser of men's clothing!

You'll write to us when you have a minute, tell us how it goes with you?

I never did.

You know what keeps bringing Billy Kahn back to me? Emily's picture on my desk. Emily will always be fortytwo. Emily died outdoors, skiing—doing what she wanted to do. That's better than caged and doped up in a hospital bed. You have to be lucky. Even in death you have to be lucky.

"Fred, you are mumbling."

"Just thinking about Dotty and Emily."

"You think too much, Fred."

"I'll have to repaint the garden sculpture."

"A little rust won't hurt your iron statues. Let it go this year. You have more important things to do."

"Like settling my oldest daughter's estate. That's all I can do for her now is fulfill her last will and testament."

"Do you have a copy of Emily's will?"

"It's in the lock box. Has been for four, five years. All sealed, not to be opened unless. I never thought I would be the one to open it."

"When are you going to do that?"

"Monday is soon enough."

"Don't forget if you need George's help . . ."

"I'll have to paint the kerosene stove or it will rust right through."

"Only in Fred Stern's yard does an old stove become garden sculpture."

"Dotty wanted to keep it. Brings back memories of Mama. Don't you remember the stove was on the back porch in Mama's summer kitchen?"

"I don't remember."

"You don't remember Mama doing the laundry in the copper boiler, rubbing, rubbing our underwear on the scrub board?"

"I remember Mama had a GE washer with a wringer on the top."

"Mama didn't get a washer until 1940."

"Fred, you have too much cluttering up your head."

"You are right, Helen. Now tell me, what do I do about it?"

"Look forward!"

"Look forward to a better tomorrow? To a new car I don't need? I have a fine car with two airbags and antilock brakes."

"To a trip. Join a tour to Turkey. Jane Miller just raved about her experiences in Turkey."

"I would rather go to Israel."

"So go to Israel."

"Maybe in October."

"Maybe Edith or Edna would like to go with you. I'll ask them."

You ask them to go for a walk with you, they don't go. Your daughters are going to take two weeks out of their committed lives to travel with their father?

"It's four years ago Emily and I went to France."

All I did was lecture Emily. You lectured Emily on the Fauve painters, on Carrière and the French symbolists, on 19thcentury French genre painting. You never stopped. Emily never asked you to go again. She chose to travel alone rather than to hear your expositions. Thank you Papa. I learned more than I ever wanted to know.

Knowledge is to be shared.

Emily never asked you to go on a trip with her again . . .

Emily has been meeting someone on her travels.

Are you sure of that, Fred?

As sure as I can be. She was so happy when she was planning her trips to the International Veterinary conferences. I would bet that she had arrangements to meet a man she cared about. Somebody who cared deeply about her. A married man, a veterinarian no doubt. American, or maybe not, who would not leave his wife—not that Emily would ever ask him to. They had their few good days together once or twice a year.

Now you are writing romances . . .

I know of other women of Emily's generation who wanted a relationship with a man on their own terms. Emily didn't want to be married. She didn't want a man around the house, into her career telling her howto and whento. She didn't need that.

You know nothing for sure.

How could I ask Emily about her most private life? A father doesn't ask a responsible adult daughter how is your love life? If there was a man in her life she surely would have at least hinted. Dad, I met a wonderful man at the conference.

Perhaps she met a woman. A younger woman. 60 percent of the veterinarians graduating today are young women. Emily was her rolemodel, a fine surgeon, a betterthanaverage horsewoman with a very successful practice. Someone to be admired, emulated. And someone to sleep with. It doesn't matter, Fred. Emily is dead.

"I'll get the door, Helen."

"Who would be at the door so early?"

"It's a quarter to nine. Could be someone from the Minyan. Helen, I'll get the door."

"Sit down, Fred! You are sitting Shiva, so sit down. I'll get the door."

David Marks. An eightyfiveyearold who looks sixtyfive. The most dependable of the Minyan. The first to arrive, the first to leave to drive the widows to their earlymorning doctor's appointments.

David's English is the amalgam of a German Hochschule and the southern slang he learned as a volunteer in the United States Army.

David pulls up the rocker, sits facing me.

"All these years I have never been in your home. It would have been better if I had come for a more joyous occasion."

"Those too will come, David. Maybe not soon but they will come. When are your grandchildren coming, David?"

"Next week, God willing. Look, I can't stay—I have to run to pick up a Challah Mrs. Katz baked this morning. Fred, on the way back, I'll bring you a Challah."

"I would like that . . . Helen, would you give David four dollars?"

"Please . . . !"

"Okay, David, next week I'll buy you a Challah."

Helen is the proper hostess. She has two glasses of grapefruit juice on a tray. Before David drinks, he speaks his prayer in Hebrew. Blessed are You our God, King of the universe, by Whose word all things came to be. David prays three times a day. Morning prayers of thanks and praise for the miracle of being freed from slavery in Egypt.

"Thank you, Mrs. Gordon."

"Helen. Call me Helen."

"It's getting warmer."

David takes off his Cubs nylon jacket, folds it into fourths, places it on the floor between the runners of the rocker.

"It was cool this morning. It almost smelled like the mountains when I was a boy at home."

Fiftytwo years in Rockville, David still speaks of the Bavarian mountains as home. Papa never spoke of Poland as home. But then Papa was only seven when he came to the United States.

"Fred, when you come back, when you get caught up . . . the next time you go to your tree farm I would like to go with you."

"Sure, David. It's better if I don't go alone. My legs, you know..."

"You still having trouble with your legs?"

"It's only arthritis."

"I see how hard it is for you to get up and down. I saw Phil help you up for the silent devotion."

"At least I am not coughing."

"You had a cough?"

"Helen, I always cough when I get a cold."

"Fred coughed for weeks. He shook the whole shul."

"It's nothing."

"It didn't sound like nothing."

"Nothing I can do about it."

"You tried, Fred?"

"I tried twenty years ago. Went to a doctor. If I remember I take my antibiotics."

"Twenty years ago?"

"It's an old story."

"What?"

"Not to worry, Helen. It's only getting worse."

"That's not funny, Fred! You're scaring me. What happened?"

"I have a damaged left lung from the fire on our bomber."

"You weren't hurt?"

"I got lung adhesions."

"You never said."

"So now you know."

"Can't you ever share, Fred?"

"Helen, don't cry . . . "

David is up, his Cubs jacket back on. "Fred, may you be comforted with all the mourners of Israel."

David out the side door.

"Helen, I didn't mean to hurt you in any way."

"That is no excuse for the way you treat me."

"You sound like Dotty."

"Don't bring Dotty into it. It's me, Helen, your only sister. You know, Fred, I never said it but you could have treated Dotty better too!"

"Not that, Helen . . . not that again!"

Chapter Nine

It's dark, sunless, dim, living under the shade of the oaks. It requires diligence and skill to grow even my thin grass lawn, no effort to grow moss. That's the rains. Wettest spring in recorded history. Any more rain, there will be record floods in July. You know from this too, Fred. The rain has to go somewhere.

"What are you reading, Fred?"

"Sienkievicz."

Helen turns over my novel, a story of 16thcentury Poland, The Fields of Glory. She returns to my open pages, reads aloud. "Meanwhile the east wind had broken the mist and driven it to the bright sun, from which the blue sky looked at them. That's not English."

"That's a translation from the Polish. Listen to this: There would be a darkness in his life which would last till the night of death should descend on him."

"Why don't you read Ludlum or Le Carré? Enjoy! Why are you reading 19th century romantic Polish novels?"

"Mama read them . . ."

"Okay, Mama read them. This novel was published in nineteen o six!"

"Sienkievicz won the Nobel Prize!"

If I Could Sleep . . .

"I give up, Fred. I give up. You make me crazy. No wonder you and Dotty . . . "

The doorbell rings, Helen hurries to answer, reappears tearing the wrappings off a bouquet with two minibronze chrysanthemums, two white carnations, and two wilted daisies. Presents it to me with a mocking flourish.

"Your weekly order from your neighborhood florist, Mr. Stern. These are ugly flowers, Fred, really ugly!"

"Better than no flowers."

"If you would spend more, you would get something you could enjoy, I could do something with. I could make a centerpiece for Sabbath dinner. What do you expect me to do with these?"

"Just put them in a vase."

"They are too ugly to put on the dinner table."

"I usually put the vase on top of the dining room buffet."

"Dotty had good taste. When Dotty was alive you spent a dollar. You weren't saving for your estate taxes."

"I don't want my death to be a burden to my daughters."

"If your money is a burden, Fred, do as George says, give it away before you die. You save fifty five percent in taxes."

"The girls each get their fair share."

"There are others you could give to. That's better than the IRS getting it all."

Helen back with the glassvase in hand, appraises her flower arrangement. "That's the best I could do. I didn't have much to work with. How much do you spend a week on cut flowers? Five dollars delivered to the door?"

"Four, Helen. The florist is a friend of mine."

"You can't be accused of being profligate."

"It's good enough."

"You could double your budget and get twice the joy of having cheerful, colorful floral varieties around the house. If you are going to

84

order flowers, get something less drab, more lasting." Helen picked at the leaves. "These were delivered half dead."

"A thing of beauty is a joy forever."

"You know from everything. I never met a man who understands so little and tells you so much. You are always telling."

"I don't tell you how to cook."

"That's true, you don't."

"See? I have a virtue."

"You're cynical and depressing. You could try to show more appreciation . . . be more sanguine."

"You won't like my new me any better."

"That's really offensive, Fred! You could try not to hurt so much."

"I never plan to hurt, it just turns out wrong."

"Try harder, Fred."

"I tried for forty three years with Dotty."

"Now you can try with your daughters."

"They complained to you?"

"Not since Dotty died. They told me plenty about how you talked to Dotty."

"Dotty never complained to me."

"Dotty was too accepting, too passive."

It will be another day without sunshine, without a sunset. Still too wet along the fenceline to plant the three snowberry, the three pink astilbe, the two trilobum viburnum, one rhododendron. Twenty dollars for delivery, sixty dollars to plant six little bushes. I'll do it myself. When I ordered I wasn't told there would be a delivery charge. You were told, it was on the estimate. It was not. Okay, deliver the bushes next week. I know it's too wet to plant. It will dry out. One or two days of sunshine is all we need.

"The sun hasn't been out since Emily's funeral."

"God is crying for Emily."

"You really believe that?"

"I don't know, Helen, I don't know."

God, from whom all goodness comes, I thank You for our lives which are in Your care, and for all that we are. Protect me. Guide me. Give me insight, give me strength to face my daily tasks with wisdom and courage . . .

"Fred, you are telling me that God knows that Emily died."

"He must."

Helen takes refuge in the kitchen, where she feels protected by the microwave, the baking oven, the roasting oven, safe from her religiousfanatic brother.

The Lord watch over you and guard you in your coming and going. He does. He did.

Mr. Stern, I am sure you have prostate cancer. Your PSA blood test is elevated and I felt a very hard knob. Doctor, how can you be so sure before you do the biopsy? I know, trust me.

The biopsy was negative, only a benign hypertrophy. Urologist never took the trouble to call me to apologize. Arrogance. Ignorance. Foolishness. Must find a wiser and gentler urologist.

Good luck!

Emily was a kind, caring veterinarian. I saw, I was with her. Saw how she cared, how faithfully she followed each case.

"You know what hurts me, Fred? When Dotty drove into that truck I thought there is a man who lost his wife. Maybe he'll finally understand. Maybe he'll learn, maybe he'll change. But you didn't."

"I had nothing to do with Dotty's death! Nothing! Dotty was driving into the setting sun. She became confused. She crossed over into the oncoming lane, hit the truck head on. That had nothing to do with me!"

"Dotty was upset with you. I know why. It was because you wouldn't listen to her!"

"Dotty was upset with me over every investment I ever made."

"Dotty had a good business head."

Alex B. Stone

"If I had listened to Dotty we would not have what we do—did."

"You would have had Dotty alive!"

Not that again. Girls, I didn't kill your mother. We had an argument. Married people argue. Maybe she was angrier than usual. Fred, every time we have an argument you end up by turning it around on me. Blaming me as if it's my fault. Dotty had cried, slammed the door. I'm going out. Where? I don't know. Out. Shopping. Bam! All I said was so I made a bad investment. I was stupid. You don't have to harp on it. You don't have to keep at me. I didn't commit a crime!

Fred, we don't need it. You are wasting your life. You were right, Dotty. I have provided eight more years of terminal care to a dying office building. Fred, I don't want you to go into a dying downtown. Any damn fool knows the downtown is dead. It's an opportunity, Dotty. We don't need it. You never let go, do you Dotty? Don't do that to me, Fred. Don't talk to me that way. You always turn things against me so it ends up that I am a scold, not that I am concerned about you. Dotty, I love you . . .

The only things Dotty was positive about was that I was a lousy investor, a worse manager, and a notalent writer. Helen is like Dotty eight years later. She is still flaying me. Dotty did not choose to drive into an oncoming truck. Suicide is against Judaism. Dotty wouldn't do suicide.

"You should have noticed that Dotty was depressed. Emily told you."

"I thought it would pass."

"You never noticed how Dotty felt. You are into yourself, only into yourself. I have never seen a more self centered man. All you do is talk about yourself. Did you ever sit down, ask Dotty, How do you feel? What did the doctor say? Dotty, tell me."

"Dotty would have told me. I didn't have to ask her."

"Dotty couldn't talk to you. That's why she started a diary. Did you ever read Dotty's diary?"

If I Could Sleep . . .

"Diaries are private! I didn't read Dotty's diary. I still haven't read it."

"When you find the guts, read Dotty's diary. You read her mail. You knew she was going for a breast biopsy, why didn't you go with her?"

"She didn't ask me to. I would have gone if she had asked me."

"Fred, you are a totally insensitive, self centered, stupid man."

When I had my back surgery, Helen, did I call you? Helen, come to Rockville. Help me! No. Went to the nursing home after the surgery. Stayed home all alone, eating sandwiches while learning to walk again.

"Fred, would you like some blintzes for lunch?"

"Blintzes would be fine."

"What would you like to drink?"

"Water or skim milk."

"Which, Fred?"

"Skim milk."

"The mail is here, more cards."

"It's like going to your own funeral, reading who made contributions in Emily's memory."

"You turn everything around to yourself, Fred. It's Emily who died."

Who did die? Don't answer Helen. Keep your thoughts for your short stories, Fred. Death the liberator. When Harvey Loewe's wife Evelyn died Harvey was freed from Evelyn's lifestyle. He took Evelyn's abstract oils off the livingroom walls, studied French nouvellecuisine and the fine art of choosing wines. Gave dinnerparties for six, for which he did the entrée en croute, the salad, the soup, the dessert and the afterdinner conversation. In three years Harvey was out of his bankerblue Brooksbrothers suits and into Europeancut Pierre Cardin, pinched at the waist styling. Harvey let his hair grow mediumlong, went on a singlescruise on the Paquet Line, returned with a Frenchspeaking widow from Milwaukee. So she didn't like Rockville and it didn't last. Cost Harvey plenty to try the widows' cruise. That's one joy he has never repeated. Last summer Harvey hiked in Tibet with the Rockville Wilderness Club. Which proves nothing at all. Nothing. Dotty wouldn't have kept me from doing what I wished. What was I going to do? Become a French Chef? Walk into the Grand Canyon with a pack on my back?

So why didn't you?

Didn't need to.

Evelyn kept Harvey as a dull, dunplumaged handbag.

It was Evelyn who showed her legs in miniskirts. I saw the Loewes at the Rockville Arts Ball, the month before Evelyn died. Looked like an ostrich—rich ostrich in gold chains. Her neck wouldn't have looked so long if she hadn't been so thin. That's what killed Evelyn Loewe. All that dieting, that healthfood, those megavitamins.

No it wasn't, Fred. You know better. She died of breastcancer like her mother and sister.

"Lunch, Fred."

"I am coming."

Rain has flooded the gazebo. Even if the sun comes out, it will be three or four days before I can sit on the porch and write. Too cold to sit outdoors. A greenslimy mold is growing under the overhang at the back door, on the back walk and on the siding. To kill the fungus add one part of bleach to ten parts of water, scrub off with a nylon broom.

"Fred, must you read the paper while we are eating?"

"The Rusty Pelican restaurant on the levee has gone bankrupt. The gambling boats were granted all the parking places on the levee. No parking, no customers."

If I Could Sleep . . .

You have a downtown office building with no parking. Fred Stern isn't going bankrupt. Fred Stern has reserves in a bank in Chicago, in a bank in South Bend. Nobody in Rockville knows how much Fred Stern has in reserves. Stern Companies are not like Olympia & York. Fred Stern can wait and wait.

Garcia Marquez wrote that love is more solid the closer we get to death. What is it you love, Fred? Your office building? Your reserves? No, I love my daughters. If you were on your deathbed they wouldn't hold your hand. Don't worry, there will be an RN, or at least a CPN by your side.

No more dying talk, Fred! You have at least fifteen more good years...

"Who did you say was coming this afternoon?"

"Bill Katz."

"Your naval aviator buddy? You going to swap war stories?"

"No. We're going to talk dirty."

"That's not funny!"

"We are going to talk about the good old days."

Ring in the good times. When Emily went off to University of Illinois. Dotty and I took off on a cartrip, Illinois to California in fourandahalf days. We had never been west of New Mexico before. Fifteen days together in a car. That's a test of love. We had a lovely time. We visited the art museums in Denver, Colorado Springs, San Francisco, Laramie, Omaha, Des Moines.

Fred, did you ask me what I would like to see?

Dotty, I thought . . .

You could have asked, Dotty, what would you like? Just once.

You are right, Dotty. I should have asked.

Dotty, I love you. Dotty, do you love me? Tell me just once . . .

I am used to you, Fred.

What kind of answer is that, Dotty? I am used to you, Fred! Do you love me? I never asked again, Dotty. That was twentyfour years ago.

Let it be. Dotty is gone, Emily is gone.

I looked forward to coming home to Dotty. It's Friday, I have a bouquet of chrysanthemums. Good Sabbath, Dotty. I hand the flowers to Dotty.

Thank you, Fred.

I'll help you set the table if you like.

Don't ask, do. I put out the tan tablecloth with napkins to match, filled the silver Kiddush cup, the wineglasses, placed the candlesticks on the buffet, put out the daily Dansk dishes and the Sabbath silver flatware, the sliced lemon in the etchedglass plate. Dotty is at the sink peeling carrots. I come up behind her, put my arms around her, kiss her ear. Good Sabbath.

You only kiss me when I am busy.

Dotty, I love you.

Dotty and I slept side by side.

Blessed be our God, King of the Universe from Whom all goodness flows. I thank You for our lives which are in Your hands. Protect us, and guide us.

I reached over, took Dotty's hand. Good night, Dotty. I kissed the top of her hand.

Good night, Fred. Sleep well.

Dotty never took my hand, never. No, never.

You were disturbing Dotty when she was reading. You knew she didn't like that.

"You want another cheese blintz?"

"No.

"I'll save it for a snack for you, Fred."

"Thanks, Helen."

Why are you dredging up such unkind memories of Dotty? That is neither fair, nor true. Dotty was your loving, caring, wife. Maybe that was fiction; a literary device; an opening paragraph to create conflict, a fairtomiddling gambit for a short story. Husband remembering a wife who left him for another. One painful memory follows another until the husband has proof sufficient that he, the jilted deserted lonely despairing husband, is now happier without his faithless wife. The reasons for a spouse of thirty years to leave have to be developed credibly, carefully.

"What are you writing, Fred? First you read the newspaper, now you write. It's bad manners to write at the lunch table."

"Just some ideas for a story."

"That's no excuse for your bad manners. I am sitting here, I made your lunch, the least you could do is talk to me."

"Writing a few words is better than watching teevee while you eat."

"You got me, Fred, but why can't we talk like two human beings?"

"We are brother and sister, not two strangers having lunch."

"I'll never understand what you say."

Dotty understood me. You know what Dotty said. She said Fred, you write about the obvious. That's why the publishers don't buy your stories. No conflict. No mystery. No sales.

"You going to take a nap after lunch?"

"I don't want to make a habit of napping. First thing I know I have to come home after lunch to nap."

"What's wrong with that?"

"I like to stay downtown until about four."

"Why? You going to miss your business opportunities?"

"Maybe I will take a nap."

"If anyone calls, I'll have them stop by about three."

"I'll be up by two thirty."

"Okay, two thirty. You saved thirty minutes for your active involved life."

Chapter Ten

"You been outside again? Nothing has changed in your backyard since yesterday. You'll catch a chill, then you'll end up coughing—coughing until you hurt. Fred, don't be getting sick on me."

"I have had my cold for this year."

"Don't get sick, Fred, so I have to stay to take care of you."

"I wouldn't do that to you, Helen.

"The Mama Tree will have to be cut down."

"Talk English, Fred. What's the mama tree?"

"That's the locust I planted in the front yard for Dotty's fiftieth birthday."

"Why take it out eighteen years later?"

"Not enough sunlight. It just never grew. The oaks shaded that struggling locust from the east sun and the roof overhang kept the west sun off. First tree I have ever had to cut down."

"It's only a tree."

"I get depressed when I kill."

"So let it live."

"It has to come out."

Cut the locust out, burn it up. That will allow the hawthorn to grow. Which tree shall live and which shall die? Good deeds, repentance and charity avert the evil decree of death. Death and resurrection through fire for your locust.

The only place for your burn pile, Fred, is out beyond the bedroom wing where I can't see it. I don't want to see your garbage I don't want to smell the stink of your fire.

Dotty, I can't garden without a burn pile.

It was a windless fall evening when I lit the newspaper under the leaves and twigs. The fire became embers that sparked redcopper and gold. When the wind puffed at the corner bedroom window, Dotty leaned out to monitor the burn pile.

You are damaging the oaks! The flames will singe the bark!

The fire is far enough away.

The grass will catch fire. I see the sparks flying. I'm not going to bed.

The fire will be out by the time we go to bed. It's just a few sparks.

I won't go to bed until you douse the fire.

I spray the fire with my garden hose until the steam rises, until the sparks fall on the ash heap, until the glowing embers are soaked charcoal.

You were out there a long time.

I didn't want you to worry. It's getting cold, Dotty. You can feel it.

You stink from smoke. You aren't going to sleep with me smelling like that.

I'll take a shower.

Fred, you never listen. I told you not to burn. I told you there was too much wind for burning.

Burn pile is now chest high, soakedwet by the spring rains. Don't know when I'll get the limbs burned. Not for weeks unless the rains stop. When I do the mosquitos will have to find another place to hatch. First we'll have gnats and then we'll have mosquitos. It was like that in 1965. It will be impossible to go out in the yard.

Alex B. Stone

"The yard is a mess."

"That's what you are worried about, Fred? The backyard? You haven't got a sense of priority."

Used to be able to see into the cemetery through the link fence. Dotty wanted the eightfoot solid pine fence to shield us, to protect us from the burials.

I can see the cemetery through the link fence!

The plantings have filled it in very nicely, Dotty.

No, Fred. I can see right into the new south part of the cemetery. I don't want to see the green burial tent, the rabbi, the mourners . . .

You knew when you built your home in Oak Hills that the Hebrew Cemetery was on the other side of the chainlink fence. More than twenty dead each year. I never thought so many would die so soon. Eight years Dotty is dead. Now Emily. Six graves left. Reservations for six. Would have been seven if I hadn't planted the pinoak.

"I'll have to trim the lower branches of the pinoak."

"What pin oak?"

"The pin oak I planted alongside Dotty's grave."

"I didn't notice."

"I had to bend my head to get under the lowest branches. I hope Dotty likes the pin oak."

"Dotty is dead."

"I like the pin oak."

"So keep it!

"Who drives a white pickup? You have a white pickup in the drive."

"That's Bill Katz."

"What does he haul?"

"Himself and Ethel to and from the Country Club."

Bill Katz matches, mixes his leisure clothes to his perfected tan. His trousers waist 36 and limegreen, his white cotton shirt with the polo emblem loose with the shoulderline low so that the sleeves reach over his elbows. Navyblue cashmere sleeveless sweater completes the effect of a gentleman golfer just back from six months of winter at his Florida condo adjoining the Weeping Willow Country Club. Homes and condos from $200thousand.

Bill follows Helen to the rocker she offers, tenders me his handshake and condolences.

"Next time I see you, Fred, it should be for happier occasions."

"Sit down, Bill. You met my sister, Helen?"

"Fred has told me so much about you."

"Thirty years of being in the same row of lockers. That's how we got to know each other. Seeing each other naked and growing fat."

Bill pats his slightest hint of belly.

"Fred doesn't get fat. Fred stops at 171 pounds for the last ten years. Me, I gain a pound a year. Fred and I are the same age, the same height, the same weight until the last few years. Now my belly is bowing out."

Drinking does make a difference. Drink is beginning to show on you, Bill. Under that tan your nose will turn capillary red.

"How are things, Fred? How are you making it?"

"Good enough."

"You look good, Fred."

"That's what I always say: Fred, for a man your age you look good."

"You look ten years younger."

"I look my age."

Helen returns with a chair from the diningroom, places it in front of the floortoceiling window wall to face Bill Katz. Bill turns to look at the paintings. "You haven't changed a painting. All are in the same place."

"Not since Dotty died."

"I told Fred to start selling off some of the paintings, move into a condo."

"I am not going to sell the house."

"Ethel and I love our condo. No yard work, no worries. We come back from Florida, I turn the key, I am home."

"Fred only spent a month in Florida."

"Fred still watches his investments."

Investments, like Papa used to say, in hopeless causes, in stupid dreams. Fred buried his money. He'll never come out of any of his investments alive. George says he'll be lucky to get thirty cents on the dollar. Fred is no businessman. He never had the belly for business. George says the only reason Fred did well was he saved Dotty's salary. Dotty was the businesswoman.

When Fred didn't listen to Dotty, when he made those investments for the social good, cheap lots for starter homes. No one wants small homes. The market is for big homes with double garages, decks and porches. Basketball hoops in the drive.

Dotty took forever to make up her mind, but she did have good taste. For a woman who never left Rockville, never went to college, she had excellent taste. Look at the Persian rug in this livingroom. Twentyfive years old. Not a sign of wear. That's quality. No one can afford a rug this size anymore. Don't remember what I paid for it, but it couldn't have cost more than 25 hundred dollars.

"Every time I come over I think of Dotty. She made you a beautiful home, Fred."

Should I sell off the paintings? That would be a service for Edith and Edna. Should sell that bucolic Walkowitz.

"Aren't you cold, Bill, going without a coat?"

"About the only clothes I have that fit are what I bought in Florida. We were going shopping for some winter things, then Ethel had to go to the doctor. It's always something."

"What's the matter, Bill?"

"She has a cold that just won't go away."

"That happens as we get older."

"If Ethel would give up her smoking. And drinking."

"That again, Bill?"

"Ethel enjoys her martini before dinner. During dinner. After dinner."

"You been flying any?"

"I didn't renew my license. I figured fifty years and I am still alive, it's time to quit."

"My husband George says that if you want to fly, rent, don't buy an airplane."

Bill laughs. "For most of my hours Uncle was paying me to fly his aircraft."

"Bill was in the Navy flying off a carrier."

"Wasn't it dangerous flying off a carrier?"

"Retirement is more dangerous." Bill laughs again. "I had more friends die from early retirement alcoholism than from enemy fire."

"And I was going to offer you a drink!"

"Not for me, Helen. I only drink with my wife.

"Fred, what's this I hear about you dropping your Country Club membership?"

"I can't walk."

"You could play off a cart."

"That's what I told him, Bill. But Fred is very stubborn. The one thing Fred really enjoys, he gives up."

"I can't walk, Helen!"

"Your back again?"

"My back and my hip."

"That's the first I heard about your hip."

"The pain started up in October. I tried to play golf in December. After nine holes, I hurt."

"You never told me."

"What is to tell, Helen? That my hip got worse and worse?"

Bill looking at the paintings again.

Alex B. Stone

"Who picked out your paintings, Fred?"

"I chose some, Dotty chose some."

"Don't let Fred fool you, Bill. He is the scholar. Just like Dad. All day long Fred does nothing but read art catalogs, art books."

Dotty chose the 1925 Guy Pène du Bois. Two workingclass girls having an afterwork drink in a Paris sidewalk café. Notice the red shoes on the girl in the grey cloth coat.

Ten years since our trip to Paris. Dotty chose our hotel on Isle St. Louis. A converted sixteenthcentury town house with an elevator for two, lobby for four. Our room above the bustling street did not become quiet until after midnight. Room so small it brought back memories of a dingy hospital cell. Gunsmoke in French and barebreasted young bodies selling healthful orange juice and Gauloise cigarettes.

That trip was the last time we bought art together. Also bought St. Louis crystal and flatware for the girls. Fred, just because we don't own a lot of crystal is no reason our daughters shouldn't have any. That's why I bought all the same patterns. When I go, the girls can have my crystal to fill in theirs.

Dotty was gone, the crystal was in the closet. Fred, distribute the crystal. Distribute Emily's crystal to Edith and Edna. Distribute Dotty's crystal to Edith and Edna.

"I always liked that painting with the cows grazing."

That, Bill, is an idyllic landscape by Walkowitz. The first of America's modernists. He and Weber were the first to go off to study in Paris. That was in the early 1900s. On the right, a pink road winds through fullfoliage green trees on its way to peace and tranquility. On the left, an innocent peasantwoman, a red bandanna tied under her chin, sits facing the viewer. Behind her, three square barns with peaked roofs, then a row of distant hills. In the center foreground, in full sun, ponies and sheep stand face into the soft midday wind. Papa found that painting in Israel. Should have asked him. Papa, what did you see in this most sentimental of paintings that I don't see? Began too late to look for Papa and Mama. Here I am, looking for Dotty and Emily.

When I remember Papa he has Helen cradled in his arms. He is walking up and down, back and forth, living room to dining room, rocking Helen, talking to her in Yiddish. Don't cry, my child, don't cry. Every time Papa comes to the dining room door he stops, turns the handle to produce the squeaksounds that stop Helen's tears.

My dad kept the Walkowitz cows in the upstairs bedroom. Dotty brought them into the living room. Walkowitz drew Isadora Duncan. Thousands of sketches of her dancing, her Grecian robes billowing behind her like a parachute. Emily liked that painting. I was going to give it to her for her birthday.

I can't remember Emily in my arms. Dotty always said I did bathe our daughters. I can't remember Emily as a baby.

"So sorry about Emily, Fred. Emily was a fun lady. You can tell about people by how they play games."

"Emily was very competitive. She liked to win."

"That's what I remember about playing golf with Emily. By gosh, Fred, by the time she was fifteen she was hitting off the men's tees. She could have been a great golfer."

"She thought golf took too much of her time. That's when she took up jogging."

"What are you going to do with her airplane?"

"George—my husband—says it's not a good time to sell airplanes with this depression on."

"What are you going to do if you can't sell it?"

"Find a charity to give it to."

"What charity would want an airplane?"

"Missionaries who save starving children in Brazilian rain forests."

"Are you serious, Fred? Give Emily's plane away? How much do you think the airplane is worth?"

"I don't know, Helen. What difference does it make?"

How much really doesn't matter for now, does it, Helen? That's next month and the month thereafter. That's another year out of my life doing for Emily.

No one else but you can do for Emily, Fred. You did for Papa, for Dotty, now for Emily.

Somebody will have to do for me. My affairs will be one expensive mess to do up cleanly.

"Fred, are you thinking of coming back to the Club?"

"First I have to decide about my hip. Replace or not to replace."

It won't get better, Fred. Just because the surgery is elective doesn't mean you shouldn't consider it. Now is the time, Fred, so you will have the most good of it. You have good health, now is the time. Consider the complications. Tenpercent get bloodclots. The lower lobe of your left lung is nonfunctional. That is an added risk. Then there is six weeks at home. You will be helpless, a onelegged man, all alone with his telephone and crutches.

"You're missed at the Club."

"I'll see, Bill. I have to decide sooner or later."

"About the surgery?"

"About the rest of my life."

"Oh, Fred! Don't be so dramatic!"

"I saw you using a cane at the funeral. When did you start that?"

"In January or February. Doctor said I should."

"You didn't tell me, Fred."

"Helen, if I told you everything, you would find out how boring my life is right here in Rockville."

"You ever see such a wet spring?"

"Never!"

Chapter Eleven

Bill has started another tale of times best forgotten.

"Fred has the most perfect golf swing. Fred could have become the club champion. All he had to do was go for it."

Helen turns to me. "I didn't know that."

"What is there to know?"

That was thirty years ago. Helen smiles, nods as if she knows the answer with no need to ask. Fred, why didn't you compete and succeed? George says striving is the American way to the top. Quitters never win.

I didn't quit. I just practiced less, didn't enter the tournaments. I cut back on golf so I could have more time with my family, with three growing daughters. Edith was taking riding lessons. Emily wanted to learn to drive my 1959 black MG with the stickshift. Around and around. Vroom . . . cough, stop, start, around and around the parkinglot of the First Baptist Church the MG lurched, infringing on Sunday afternoon naptime. Me beside Emily in the redleather bucketseats until someone called the police. Miss, do you have a license? That's pretty erratic driving. Emily smiled, presented her license. My father was teaching me to drive a stickshift.

I didn't recognize you, Mr. Stern. Not in those shorts and sweat shirt.

The MG with dual carburetors was not a car for Western Illinois's changeable weather. Toocold winters, toowet springs.

I am not pushing you and your dream machine out of the driveway! Call the AAA!.

If I Could Sleep . . .

Just one more time, Dotty . . .

I have had eight years with your midlife crisis and your sportscar. That's enough!

Dotty always chose large, sensible cars. Her first was a robinegg blue 1954 Olds fourdoor. I taught Dotty to drive on the country roads south of Rockville. Wouldn't you know, that was one time she didn't tell me You can do better, Fred, you just don't try hard enough!

I do for everyone. I buried the dead, provided dowries for my daughters, studied Torah, gave charity. It was never enough. No matter how much I give, the Community's needs become greater and greater as we become fewer and fewer. My charities were the one thing Dotty didn't complain about.

Bill is talking to Helen. "I have not been in the cemetery since Dotty's funeral. I don't do funerals."

Helen, please don't tell Bill what a good deed it is to bury the dead. Bill buried his dead off the carrier's deck. In two years Bill prayed at a lifetime of funerals.

"Thank you for coming, Bill."

"It's the least thing I could do for you and Emily. I'm going to miss Emily. Not too many daughters go to lunch with their father and his old buddies."

Emily was interested. What was it like during the war? Bill, what was it like to shoot down Japanese airmen?, or Dad, how could you drop bombs on children and civilians? The only answer she got from Bill was When I was stationed in Pensacola, Ethel found a furnished basement apartment, which was not so unusual a place to live in then because of the housing shortage. What was unusual was that the door to the bathroom, which was in a corner of the living room, had been cut off about two thirds of the way up to allow for ventilation. If we had company, Ethel wouldn't let me use the bowl, so I would excuse myself. Ethel is almost out of cigarettes. I would run down to the gasstation, use their washroom and buy a pack of Lucky Strike. When

I shipped out, Ethel had enough cigarettes for the next six months.

Dad, what was it like for you and Mom when you came back from the Airforce?

We were the lucky ones. We rented Herb Miller's bungalow from his dad. You remember Nathan Miller who ran the furniture store on Thirdavenue? Herb was in the armored, in the tankcorps. He died somewhere in Germany. A sniper's bullet through his forehead. His wife Sally went back to Northern Illinois to Dekalb. So when Nathan heard we needed a place to live he rented Herb's bungalow to us. We were lucky. We lived there until Ralph, the younger son, came home from the Navy and wanted to get married. Can you hear me laugh? Nathan Miller was afraid I wouldn't give up the house to Ralph. Of course we would have. Nathan served us a lawyer letter and a legal dispossess notice. That frightened your mother more than having to go through the spiderwebs to stoke the coal furnace. I still have Herb's Complete Conrad Reader that we found in the attic.

From this fourhundredfamily Rockville congregation eleven young men died in World War II. I was the fortunate one. I came home. Fortyeight years later the Rabbi doesn't have a list of the dead to read on Memorial Day.

"I see the cemetery has a new section."

"The only growth industry in town."

"Fred, did you know my sister Pauline insisted that she and Matt sell their house and retire to a condo in Iowa City?"

"It is not a good time to sell a home in Rockville. Why would your sister..."

Helen knows why, but she has to ask Bill.

"After all, you are here and after all these years moving is so disruptive..."

Gleefully, she will discuss Bill's response with me when Bill leaves.

"Too many old people in Rockville."

No question the cultural life is more varied in Iowa City. Because of the university, opera, dance, theater, lectures, foreign flicks. The last movietheater in Rockville that showed artfilms went out of business 30 years ago. Now there is only the 8 cinema complex showing straight American sex and violence. Stallone, Eastwood and Schwarzenegger.

"When are you going back to your swimming?"

"Monday."

"I couldn't live here all alone. Too big a house to take care of."

"Fred loves yard work. Has Fred shown you through his sculpture garden?"

A rustedthrough tin QuickMeal kerosene stove built in 1925. A bronze sundial with a broken style that sits in the shade between the Amur maple and the nonflowering lilacbush. So old it stays up only because it has the chainlink fence to lean on as it searches blindly for the sun. Rotting picnictable that only the squirrels use now and then for quarrelling and cracking acorns.

"I do enjoy yard work."

"With your back, you don't need it."

"The picnic table was a gift from Emily."

"Emily bought you the Weber grill. You don't use that either."

"Charcoal broiled food causes stomach cancer."

"At your age, Fred, you don't have to worry."

"I know, Helen. I won't live long enough to be affected."

"Tell him, Bill, tell him to learn to use the grill. Tell him how easy it is to do hamburgers."

"You got a lot of condolence cards."

Helen has lined up the condolence cards on the dining room buffet like it was Hanukah or Rosh Hashana for everyone to see how many still remember the Sterns. Helen leaves I throw the cards out.

"Fred goes to dinner with us every Tuesday."

"How long has that been going on? Fred never told me."

"For years."

"Any new good restaurants in town?"

"We go to Bishop's Cafeteria."

"That figures. All you can eat for four ninety nine?

"I like the corn bread."

"Don't you know that it's full of fat, sugar and salt?"

"Don't worry, Helen. I am taking my blood pressure pills."

"How is your cholesterol doing, Fred? You getting your blood tested?"

"It's raining again."

"I made a point of seeing Fred in Florida. I wanted him to stay longer, come over to Lakeland, spend four, five days with us."

"I wanted to get home by February tenth."

"What do you have to do in Rockville that can't wait until March tenth?"

The Stern lecture in Judaica, the spring cultural event at B'nai Jacob. How would it look if Fred Stern missed Professor Sheldon Abram's discourse on the linguistics of Yiddish?

The audience twelve intellectuals over seventyfour years of age, the Rabbi, the Hazzan and a newspaper reporter from the Rockville Echo Herald. Dr. Sheldon Abrams of the University of Chicago discussed the German, Slavic, Hebrew origins of Yiddish, a language no one in Rockville speaks anymore, that only four nodding heads can write and only one, the Rabbi, still reads. In his monthly Yiddish literary magazine the Zukunft.

"I didn't see Edith or Edna. How are they doing?"

"Still busily into their careers."

"What is Edna doing?"

"Politics. Edna has her eye on a political career. She is determined to get to Washington." Edna building feminist friendship circles, support networks, women supporting unwed mothers with children, unwed mothers who gave up their children, mothers by choice without fathers, lesbians who want to create a gay press to publish their insights into their newly discovered sexual awareness, women for equal rights, women for choice, women for women's literature.

Edna always shared more with her girlfriends than she did with any of her family.

Dotty, how did we fail Edna that she has turned to friends, to strangers for support? Edna more concerned about her girlfriends than she is about her family?

Fred, I was there for her. If you want to think we failed her, that is your guilttrip, not mine. Every child has parents that fail them. Fred, my mother died young. So she failed me.

You had me, Dotty.

Don't get me started on that, Fred.

Kiss me, Dotty. Put your arms around me and hold me tight. Kiss me once, kiss me twice, kiss me once again. It has been a long, long, time.

Fred, there are questions you shouldn't ask.

Dotty, love me, kiss me. Dotty, I have learned to wait.

Fred, it is I who have been waiting . . .

Bill Katz has got up and is making motions to go. Bill, you have done your duty. You have stayed long enough. Go home, Ethel needs you. Hide the vodka. Insist she drink straight orangejuice. Ethel still looks good, her face isn't blotching. Must be her makeup base that covers the aging.

We are all different. One vodka I am sick all of the next day. One glass of wine puts me to sleep for four hours. Helen and George have an oldfashioned Manhattan before dinner. How quaint. The trendy drink light. Just a little Perrier or Evian please. A sip of Korbel champagne or Buena Vista Chardonnay for special occasions only.

"Bill, do you and Ethel want to come to Sabbath dinner?" That's not fair to Helen. I surely didn't intend to offend Helen.

Alex B. Stone

"Yes, do come. It would be nice to have company for Sabbath dinner."

Bill and Ethel better company than I. Better than dining alone with your dour brother.

Helen Gordon's Sabbath dinner: lean lambstew with carrots, accompanied by a salad of romaine lettuce, tomatoes cucumbers and redpepper served without dressing. Vinegar and oil available by special request. Afterwards tea and lemon. Healthful, nutritious, lowfat, lowsalt. I will say the blessings over the candles. In a household without a woman, a man may perform the blessings that welcome the Sabbath. Maybe Helen will bless the candles. I'll ask her to. The Gordons don't light candles, don't do blessings.

"I'll see how Ethel feels."

Ethel only drinks at home.

"Bill, please call me tonight, let me know how Ethel is feeling."

"I'll walk you to the door."

"Don't get up, Fred."

"I've been sitting long enough."

"You will miss Emily."

I nod. I have missed Emily since she went down to State. Our firstborn, from whom we demanded excellence, love, obedience, hugs and kisses.

"Emily achieved a great deal in her short life."

"A terrible loss, Fred. You know what I thought when I was sitting here? I don't know how you are going to manage. First Dotty and now Emily."

"Ayn brira. No choice."

"Fred, if you need me . . . you know. I can find my own way out."

"I'll go with you. I want to go outside for a minute."

"If you go out, take a jacket!"

Under the oak the doves are eating the thistle that fell from the finch feeder.

る

If I Could Sleep . . .

"What did you say, Fred?"

"I said it's raining again. It's the wettest spring since nineteen sixtyfive. This keeps up the Corps of Engineers will have to stop the river traffic."

"It would be nice to have Bill and Ethel for Sabbath dinner."

You remember, Helen, how Papa always brought home Sabbath guests for Mama to feed? In those days we had travelling salesmen coming to services. Every Friday Night dinner was the same as the Sabbath before and the one before that. Chickensoup, boiled chicken, canned purpleplums for dessert, tea with lemon, homebaked Challah and Manischewitz Concord wine for the Kiddush.

"Yes, Helen, it would be nice to have the Katzes for Sabbath dinner. Thank you, Helen, thank you."

Chapter Twelve

Thursday. Only two more days.

"Fred, do you know how much junk you have in your garage? It's an obstacle course to get to your garbage can."

"Tomorrow is garbage day. I'll take the cans out."

"You ever throw anything out?"

"What's for lunch?"

"I thought you only wanted a salad."

"Salad would be fine."

"Fred, you don't hear a thing I am saying to you. Let me throw some of that junk out!"

I hear you, Helen. I know what is where in the garage. On the west wall, in the corner closest to the garagedoor, a Lawnboy mower that needs the two frontwheels replaced and the blade sharpened, which I will do when Value Hardware offers the $38.00 spring special fixup. Going north, flowerpots for the redandpink impatiens that will garland the oak trees. Fourteen pots for the oaks that shade the front door, two pots to define the end of the walk, two pots at the front door, five or six at the base of the backdoor oak to be seen from the gazebo and the dining room. Continuing north along the west wall is my discarded green vinyl golfbag with the tornfree battered pockets. In the golfbag is a bamboo leafrake, one narrow metal leafrake, one wider metal twigrake, a twopronged hoe, a dandelion cutter, a short flagpole. In the pocket, a fourteeninch stainlesssteel postmortem knife.

Next, standing, leaning on the wall, in my brown golf carrybag, my graphiteshaft golfclubs with the builtup padded grips for my arthritic hands, bought years ago at a yearend sale at a savings of 50%. Then, a halfgallon of residual insect spray to wither, shrink, kill the woodroaches spiders and beetles that so frightened Dotty. To be used only in a predawn stupor, when I crackle, pop the vermin on the kitchen floor.

In the northwest corner, a thirtyyearold rotary leafrake with the original yellow nylon catcher half torn from the metal frame. On the topmost shelf of the north wall a toboggan for five—father, mother, three daughters.

Dotty so appealing in her belted midcalflength camelhair coat, the girls in jeans and heavy sweaters worn over winter woollens. Hands tight on the rope I steer the toboggan. Dotty has her arms and legs around me. Behind her Edith and Edna cling to eachother and Dorothy. Emily pushes us over the crest, jumps on, wraps herself around her sisters, grips the side cordings. We whiz, whoosh down the bluff. The new snow sprays, rises, sticks to my sunglasses. At the bottom of the bluff we coast, bump over the flat, buffered to a tumbling stop by the strawfilled roadside ditch that keeps us from skittering onto Illinois Highway 84. Dotty and the girls laughing, trailing behind, I pull the toboggan back up the bluff. Down was easy, up not too difficult either.

Hasn't been a public tobogganslide in Rock County in thirty, forty years. Something to do with too dangerous and public liability.

Emily kept her iceskates in the utilityroom closet with her abandoned woodframe tennis racquet. Till Dotty told her Emily you have a place of your own now. I have a couple of boxes of your things all ready for you to take. Dotty packed, taped, labelled the contents. Rockville High Yearbooks, University of Illinois Notes, Art History,

Alex B. Stone

Chemistry, English Lit. Three long partydresses, one blue, one green, one Hawaii print. Dotty folding the plastic garmentbag into the trunk of Emily's Celica. Wedged the boxes behind her seat.

It was Emily's idea to take her books. Emily took her Holy Days Prayerbook, the Chumash given to her at her Bat Mitzva, a collection of contemporary American short stories and a manuscript copy of my Rockville Tales.

Helen's orderly mind is evident in how she sorted my mail. The white and blue utilitybills for the Florida condo are in front of the Midwest Trust transaction reports, followed by the businesssize envelopes—appeals, charities, causes, Biblical Archeology, Alumni Travel. Last, two large brown envelopes, one from Rockville Arts, the other from Explorer Expeditions, who offer to take me on a small, slow boat to the head of the Orinoco River so that I may view native tribes losing their lifenurturing rainforest habitat to earthmurdering mining and lumbering interests.

"You still giving to Papa's charities?"
"Some."
"George says that—"
"It's my money."
"But Papa's causes?"
"So?"
"You live in the past."
"I do the best I can."
"You throw away your money on things you aren't even interested in. Why didn't you develop your own interests?"
"Those are my interests."
"When was the last time you were in Berkeley at the Magnes Museum?"
"Ten, fifteen years ago. I don't remember."

"But this says you are a member!"

"I support Jewish museums. You expect Methodists to support Jewish museums?"

"You always turn it around. Now it's my fault because I think you should develop a life of your own."

"The expression, Helen, is: Get a life!"

"Okay: Get a life! . . . Why are you laughing at me, Fred?"

"I just thought of that old line where the comedian says, You call this living?'"

"I don't understand."

"Believe me, Helen, I don't understand how or why I am living or what I am doing in Rockville. Papa had a reason. Papa came to Rockville to practice veterinary medicine. I could have done better in a larger community, but I stayed in Rockville."

"You sound like Papa."

"I am Papa."

"Fred!"

"That's why I support museums, go to the Stern lectures at Rockville College, because I am Papa."

"All I said was that you should throw some of the junk out of your garage."

"You read my mail?"

"I sorted your mail. I took out the condolence cards. They were addressed to the Stern family. I am family. I am your sister."

"You want a toboggan?"

"Put it in the rummage. Fred, for your own sake, do something. Get your hip replaced. It won't get better. Six months out of your life, then you'll golf, walk on the beach in Sanibel. You used to like that."

A cruise, dancing on the moonlit deck with the widows. A predatory widow will rope me. Do a premarital agreement. Protect yourself. Take a fling.

"I have a date for the hip replacement surgery. June twentythird."

"Congratulations! Why didn't you tell me? I could come out and help you."

"We'll see. Two or three weeks after the surgery would be helpful."

"It will do wonders for you, Fred."

It will change your life, Fred. Remove the pain in your hip. All I'll have left is the pain in my back, the pain in my shoulders, in my wrists. It's elective surgery, Mr. Stern, but that doesn't mean there's no risk. Tenpercent of our patients develop bloodclots. Have you ever had bloodclots, Mr. Stern? Your ankles are swollen, Mr. Stern. Dorothy Glass died from a bloodclot. She was only sixtytwo. Abe Glass's wife. You remember her, Helen?

"You aren't going to get rid of some of the junk in the garage? Do you know how many corrugated boxes you have?"

"How many, Helen?"

"That's not funny."

"Don't you have anything better to do than to count my boxes?"

"I could help you throw things out, Fred. You have enough folded boxes to move your entire household."

"Dotty started saving the boxes so that all Edith and Edna will have to do is fill them up with our linens, silver and crystal and ship them out."

Maybe Dotty thought we would die together and then all would be ready. I can't remember where Dotty got all those boxes. I took them apart, stood them flat upright.

"The cartons don't really take up all that much room."

"Fred, I can't get around your car."

"The cartons act as bumpers so that I can't hit the toy box with my car."

"Saving the toy box for whom and why?"

I am saving the toy box for my first grandchild. The first grandchild gets the handmade toybox. The restored old wagon . . . the second grandchild should get the wagon. I pulled the girls in that wagon. Faster, faster, Papa! Why did you have the wagon repainted, the wheels replaced? I thought, like in the prayerbook. From generation to generation . . .

You have not been a fortunate man. Lucky to have survived, but that's all. No grandchildren to play basketball with. The backboard is rotten, cracked through. So is the gazebo door. So is the fascia under the raingutter.

I'll take Charlie off the downtown officebuilding, put him to fixing up the house. It's been raining for months. Charlie has the roofleaks to repair. Mister Stern, we need a new roof. You have been patching for twelve years. I know, Charlie, I know. It has never rained this much in the history of the Mississippi River Valley. Charlie can't keep up with the downtown repairs. How can he help you at home? It only leaks when it rains. Get a new roof. Dig into your reserves. I'll sell out. Let someone else fight the storms, the floods, the OSHA regulations. Sell. Sell!

At what price? At any price. Quit! Rockville is finished. Leave. Where shall I go? Go live with Edna? With Edna, or move closer to Helen and George. George isn't all that bad. George knows everything I used to know.

"Helen, you are right. I should . . . ."

"Fred, there is a little round man with a short beard."

"He drive up in a red sportscar?"

"How did you know?"

"It's Hazzan Silver with the golden voice."

"It's lunch time. Who comes to pay a condolence call at lunch time?"

"Maybe he wants you to ask him to lunch."

"Do you want me to?"

"Whatever you like, Helen."

"He is your friend. I'll do what you wish."

"Bernie Silver is our hazzan. He hasn't made a friend in the two years he has been here."

"He is making his condolence call. He didn't have to . . ."

"The religious committee made him."

"That's because you are a big giver. You sit, Fred. I'll get the door."

"Hazzan Silver. Fred has told me so much about you. I cried when I heard the sorrow in your Kayl Melech Rachomim.

"I get plenty of practice. Twenty eight funerals last year."

Bernie unwraps his blue woollen boa from his neck, opens his blue insulated kneelength jacket, reveals his redflannel shirt open to the third button. Through the black forest of his chesthair a hammeredgold spreadwing eagle soars on a gold chain. Must be some social significance to his jewelry. A freedom emblem. A Nativeamerican totem. A lodge insignia. It's Bernie's personal adornment and none of your business. Two months more and Bernie is gone. At least he isn't wearing an earring . . . Every two years another hazzan. The next one will be younger, wear a designer beard and call himself Cantor.

"We were just sitting down for our lunch. Just a salad, that's all Fred ever eats for lunch. A salad with matzo."

"Not many in Rockville keeping kosher."

"We don't mix meat and dairy products, but we don't have separate dishes for meat and dairy. Believe me, Mr. Silver, my brother is the only one I know who changes his dishes for Passover."

"For my matzo sandwiches."

"Will you join us for lunch?"

Bernie hesitates like a man in a hurry who rushes out the back door after each service.

"You have to eat lunch anyway," Helen coaxes.

Bernie doesn't say yes. Bernie doesn't say no. The Hazzan follows us into the dining room. Helen has set an extra service opposite herself.

"Fred drinks tea and lemon."

"Do you have a diet drink?"

Bernie needs more exercise. Dieting won't help him lose his belly. Thirtyfive years old and forty pounds overweight. When I was thirtyfive I worked day and night, didn't have the time to get fat. Hazzans have more choices. Even our gloomy Hazzan with the bird around his neck has other choices besides Rockville. If Bernie had so many choices he wouldn't have come to Rockville. He came because of riverboat gambling. Every night he is out on the riverboats, gambling. No, working as a blackjack dealer. That would explain why he is always late for the morning Minyan. Also explains why he yawns, dozes, rushes through the Torah readings. So he can go back to bed. That's why the funerals disturb him. They interfere with his afternoon naps.

"Blessed be our God who brings forth bread from the earth".

Bernie answers Amen. Helen looks at me quizzically, shrugs her shoulders in resignation. I wouldn't want our hazzan to think that I don't bless our food. Mine usually is silent prayer, but with company how would Bernie know how thankful I am for what the good Lord has given us.

"It's a beautiful house, Mr. Stern."

"A very easy house to live in."

"If you have a family to share it with . . . I'm sorry, Mr. Stern, I didn't mean . . ."

"It's alright, Hazzan."

"There are two baths and two bedrooms downstairs."

"Isn't it painful for you to sit on the low stool?"

"Not too bad."

"Nobody sits Shiva anymore, let alone sit on a low stool wearing house slippers."

I shave, I shower, I change my clothes, I go outside. Didn't tear the lapel of my jacket. Didn't tear the pocket on my shirt. Rockville is not an orthodox community. Some of us are simply more observant than others. Traditions change very slowly in Western Illinois along the Mississippi—but they are changing. Emily and Dotty still buried in a woman's row, though. Between two women they never even knew. Segregated even in death. Coordinates fixed forever by the accident of death. My funeral will be from the Reformed Temple, not from B'nai Jacob. I fooled the religious committee. They said No funerals may be conducted in our sanctuary. I fooled them. I joined the Temple in Davenport, Iowa. There will be two eulogies. One from the Rabbi of B'nai Jacob, one from the Rabbi of the Temple.

You went to a lot of planning, Fred. Surgery coming up. Had to plan ahead. Haven't written my obituary just yet. Not planning to, either. At least not very soon. Maybe one day.

The New York Times does beautiful obits. Fred, you want an obit in the New York Times you'll have to pay for it by the classified inch. Unless Rockville Tales is published to great reviews, becomes a bestseller, wins the National Book Award. Then they'll give it to me for free. Fanfare; exit Fred Stern.

Raspberry.

"So you'd like to have a family, Hazzan Silver?"

"It's not that easy, Mrs. Stern."

"Gordon."

"I'm sorry. Mrs. Gordon. Of course."

"Not so easy why?"

"You know how it is. A lady wants a husband with a steady job. A synagogue wants a hazzan with a steady wife."

"Oh, I'm sure a strong young man with a voice like yours . . . "

"And a physique like mine. Why do you think they hired me? You think they couldn't find a better voice? Anyway, my contract is almost up."

"And then?"

"Then? Then I don't know. Maybe law."

"I think you'd make a fine lawyer."

"It says in the Bible, Male and female He created them. Your other half is somewhere out there waiting for you, looking for you. She'd never guess you've been hiding out here in Rockville."

"Thank you Mr. Stern. I hope you're right."

"More salad, Hazzan?"

"Thank you, I have to go."

"Where are you rushing?"

"You'll probably think this is awfully funny, but I forgot I was supposed to meet someone for lunch. I think I can still catch them. I guess it felt so good to be in a real home, I plain forgot all about it."

"If you want to get married, young man, you'll have to learn not to keep the ladies waiting."

"Oh no! It's not a date. I'm supposed to meet my study partner from law school."

"Law school? You're in law school?"

"Yes, but please don't tell anybody. It's supposed to be a secret. It could hurt my chances if something really good came up for a hazzan. I have to run. Thank you for the salad. Sorry for your loss, Mr. Stern. May God comfort you among the mourners of Zion and Jerusalem! Good bye . . . "

Have some more salad, Fred?

Chapter Thirteen

"This would be a good time for you to nap."

"I'll lie down and read."

"Try to fall asleep, you have to try."

"Why are you looking at me that way?"

"You sounded exactly like Dotty. The last few years all I heard was Fred you can do better! I must have been a disappointment to Dotty."

"Dotty was disappointed in more than you, Fred, or she wouldn't have committed suicide."

"Helen, will you stop this nonsense about . . ."

"All right, Fred. Have it your way. Dotty didn't commit suicide."

Dotty's calendar was full of To Do notes. Buy Chanukah gifts for the girls. Dotty had to find the same gift for each daughter. Do you realize how difficult that is? In August we were in Iowa City at Land's End outlet shop. Dotty bought four cottonknit coverups—a green, a purple, a yellow, a pumpkin. I'll keep this purple for myself. It's ideal for the Sanibel beach. Why would Dotty buy December beachwear in August and then commit suicide in September?

"I'm still going into her dressing room and clean out her shoes. You can throw them out or give them to rummage but you are going to do something."

If I Could Sleep . . .

Dotty's shoes that she didn't wear but saved because They May Become Fashionable Again. Red shoes with square heels, black patentleather pumps with pointed toes, brownandwhite spectators she wore twice to a countryclub luncheon twenty years ago.

"You are right, Helen."

"Why don't you listen to me?"

"You sound like Dotty."

Why don't you listen? I have never met a man so arrogant, so sure of himself and so wrong!

Dotty, that's my generation, it's my training. To decide, to reach decisions good or bad. I was taught to decide.

Decided to retreat so that the North Koreans couldn't outflank us. Because we retreated, our airfield was not captured. In four months we were able to reorganize, to fight again. For that, on the 19th of October at Pyong Yang, our Airforce unit received the General's commendation.

Dotty, not all my decisions were poor. Most had to have been good or at least adequate.

Fred, you did not consider the risk. The price you had to pay for your decisions.

Perhaps I needed the rush of the struggle, the challenge. Perhaps you were right, Dotty. I am sure you were right. Dotty, I am truly sorry for the grief I caused you, for the sorrow I brought to your life. What I did I didn't do it to hurt you. I thought it was in our best interest. I just couldn't think of working for a salary in a time when America needed affordable housing. When so many needed homes and apartments. Dotty, I built housing for the handicapped, for the elderly!

We didn't need it, Fred. You always forget your grief, the grief you gave me.

There was no one else who was willing to do what we did. Dotty, don't you remember why we began to build? It was to fill a social need. There was no rental housing in Rockville! Dotty, you should have been proud. Dotty, we were the first. We succeeded against all the gloomy predictions. No money, no experience, no political connections. No expertise in multifamily finance. We created! Onehundredandsixtyfour homes for families with children, for minorities, for the handicapped. You and me, we provided low cost, low density, safe, sound shelter. You should be proud, Dotty. We were the first.

What did you get for your deeds of lovingkindness?

We did good, Dotty. That's enough.

Everything has a price, Fred. The price you paid was too high. You ran the housing for eighteen years. Did you ever make a penny? No, just grief and anxiety.

We were young, Dotty. This was our challenge. We conquered the City Council, the zoning commission, the complaining neighbors, the HUD delays.

You left the University for what? To struggle?

You are right, Dotty.

When we embarked for Korea, the band played Stars and Stripes Forever. Eyes right we passed in review, dipped our regimental pennants. The General saluted; I returned the salute. The 24th Division was the first into South Korea. We were there, right behind them. We retreated November 25th when the Chinese Field Army began to infiltrate behind our lines putting up roadblocks that would have trapped us like animals. We were lucky not to be in a forward position. We moved east which prevented the Chinese from cutting our escape routes to the south.

You have to be tough, stupid and brave to be first. We didn't know the mortgage banks would cheat us, that HUD would not permit us to increase the rents to offset our rising costs.

Our problems with the housing began when the HUD rent regulators retreated into their bureaucratic burrows. They stonewalled us. I made the correct decision. When there was insufficient funds to pay the mortgage and to maintain the property, I maintained the property.

You ended up with so much debt you finally lost the housing.

Yes, but we didn't go bankrupt. We could have filed for bankruptcy and pocketed the rental income. We put every penny back to maintain and replace.

You, with your social responsibilities, Fred. You lost the housing anyway. Fred Stern, you are a man of integrity. The only man of integrity I ever met who chose to keep up his property instead of harvesting it. And then abandon it for HUD to sell at auction for ten cents on the dollar.

Provide dowries for orphans, charity for the poor, study Torah, bury the dead. That is what is demanded of us. We made a living, didn't we? and had a sense of fulfilment, too. Spiritually rewarding. Hundreds came to our 10thanniversary open house. Thank you for caring, Mr. Stern. Mrs. Stern, I would like to thank you, too.

No thanks necessary.

We built the housing for the elderly with no thought of financial reward. One project turns out well, another drains and drains our energy and hope.

Our daughters did not come to our 10thanniversary party at the housing for the elderly. Emily had her practice, Edna and Edith had their own causes. I did ask them to attend. Why, Dad? To hear from politicians how wonderful you are? To eat greasy friedchicken? To toast my parents with cheap André American champagne?

The girls did come to Rockville College for the dedication of the Stern Art Library. Maybe thumbing through artbooks is less of a stigma than owning a fivestorey highrise for the elderly.

"Fred, there is a Labrador retriever running loose in your yard."

"That's the neighbor's pup."

"He shouldn't run loose. He's dumping on your hydrangea bush!"

Our Boston Terrier Suzy was Emily's dog. Smartest dog we ever had. When she wanted me to take her for a walk (that was after Emily had gone off to Champaign), Suzy would bring me her leash. If we didn't take her out, she'd run out. Suzy would wait for the doorbell to ring, wait until the door was open, then she'd dart between our legs and down the street.

That's how it happened. She darted across the street, was hit by a passing car. She came home, wagged her tail, went to her bed in the utility room and quietly gently died from a ruptured spleen.

What are you going to tell Emily?

I'll tell her the truth.

If you had taken Suzy for her walk Suzy wouldn't have . . .

If Grandma had wheels she would have been a trolley car!

You promised Emily that you would take Suzy for her aftersupper walk!

I was going to, as soon as I finished the newspaper. Patience is a virtue, even in dogs.

"Fred, that dog is in your back yard!"

"He'll go home."

"He will kill your hydrangea."

Of so many, there is only one hydrangea left on the fenceline.

"Nothing is forever, Helen. It's been more than twenty years since I put in the hydrangeas. How long can hydrangeas that don't feel the sun live?"

Dogs can live to be fifteen or sixteen or seventeen. The smallthin dogs live longest. Thin old men live longer. You, Fred, are not too fat, but neither are you thin. Not old either. Your arms are too thin. Your life expectancy is 16 years and 6 months.

"Fred, what are you going to do with the books you have piled in the garage? You had better do something. The way it's been raining, they will be all mold."

We twelveyearold Jewish boys of the first immigrant generation read Ralph Henry Barbour's Tales of New England College Life.

If I Could Sleep . . .

Lastminute victories on the playing fields of old Siwash U. Jack Armstrong, the Allamerican upper class WASP boy, wins all. The girl, the job on Wall Street.

Tom Swift, a son of the lower classes, not quite workingclass but certainly not patrician. Found his fortune in industrial America. Tom Swift and his washing machine. Tom Swift and his house on wheels.

"Those are my books of sixty years ago. They are not doing any harm in the garage."

"When you go you know what the girls are going to do with all your garbage? Throw it out."

"Each one of those Tom Swifts is worth three dollars."

"Fred! A man of your means."

"I promise, Helen, I'll give my books to the Rockville Library so they can sell them."

"A quarter a piece is what they'll get. Fred, you remember when Grandpa retired from the factory? His boss gave him a bottle of champagne."

"So?"

"You remember what happened? Grandpa saved the champagne for fifteen years for his eightieth birthday and—you were there—and when he opened it it was vinegar."

"Books don't spoil."

"They'll mold, smell bad, stink!"

"I promise, Helen."

"Promise what?"

"I'll get to the garage."

"The only clean thing in the garage is your car."

"Cleanliness is next to godliness."

"Fred, you have to think of your future. Do something about it."

"I will."

"I know you. The minute you drop me off at the airport you'll be back to your old ways. You were always so clean. I admired that in you. Look at yourself now."

"That's what I learned in the Air Force, Helen, to polish my shoes and change my underwear every day. Don't forget I was an officer and a gentleman."

"I am serious! Look at yourself, Fred. How long has it been since you looked at yourself?"

"I'm sitting Shiva, Helen."

"How long has it been since you trimmed your moustache?"

"I take a shower every morning. I change the sheets every Sunday."

"I don't know how to say it, Fred."

"Say it, Helen, you will anyway."

"You look unkempt!"

"Not dirty?"

"That's nothing to laugh about, Fred. Why are you laughing?"

"Who is looking at me?"

"There are plenty of fine looking widows who would look at you if you gave them a chance."

"You are right, Helen. Better a wife to take care of me than to be dependent on my children."

"So?"

"When the time comes when I need help, I'll call the visiting nurses."

"Aren't you lonely?"

"Not now."

"Were you ever? Surely you were when Dotty died."

Emily called me every weekend Saturday night or Sunday. Papa, you okay?

Doing good, Emily.

What did the doctor say?

Doing good, Emily. No sense unloading on your children.

Emily will never call again. Emily is gone, like Dotty, gone forever. Why don't you cry, Fred? Cry. I wish I could. I would if I could. My heart cries, my soul cries, my body aches. My eyes are dry.

It's raining again. No one will visit until the rain stops.

Face it, Fred. You have to face Emily's death. Emily is gone, dead at fortytwo and on Monday you'll have to face her will. I'd rather not. Emily chose you as executor, you accepted. Reluctantly. I am too old, Emily, choose a friend, a young friend.

There is no one I would rather trust than you.

I'm not wise, Emily. Sometimes I wasn't forthright with your mother. I'd never tell her we were going into another business venture until all she had to do was sign. Your mother never walked away from me. She never walked out on a signing. She signed, and waited, and screamed at me in the privacy of our home.

Chapter Fourteen

On my stool, clipboard on my lap, I write. Thank you for thinking of me in my sorrow. Thank you for supporting me in my loss. Your donation to remember Emily is kind, generous, thoughtful, is appreciated.

Emily, gone, buried beside Dotty. Both died without medical attention. Dotty who believed male doctors don't pay attention to women. Fred, women have special needs . . .

Dotty didn't receive any more support from her she doctor than from her he doctor. Mrs. Stern, we have to do a second smear. The cells are normal, but in view of your uterine bleeding, we should do a deeancee . . .

Poor Dotty, if it wasn't one thing, it was another. Thinking about the deeancee, she could have been distracted. Hers was only a slight discharge for a few days. The bleeding had stopped. Dotty was so relieved.

Dotty was about to call Dr. Fuller.

Call Dr. Fuller was on Dotty's calendar!

Of course she didn't commit suicide! Dotty became confused for that one moment. For that one moment when she crossed into the oncoming lane to pass, to get around the cementtruck dripping water and shedding cement dust on her new opalblue Lincoln. Look at

Dotty's calendar. See for yourself. The next week we had scheduled a taxplanning visit to the accountants.

Mr. James, our accountant, was Dotty's ally. Dorothy, I agree with you. Mr. Stern should sell. I am sure Mr. Stern understands. I am sure Mr. Stern will sell when the opportunity presents itself.

Your gift to Emily's memorial fund at Kansas State College of Veterinary Medicine will be a perpetual memorial. Thank you for your condolences. So many of Emily's classmates have called and written to me during these days of mourning. It is comforting to be remembered.

"Fred, why are you sitting like that all hunched over? You are going to end up with a broken back."

"Help me up. I need to stretch."

The humidity gauge under the overhang shows 94. In the sun the thermometer registers 80.

"I'm going out, Helen."

Downed oaklimb on the groundcover. Pick it up, add it to the brush burn pile.

Helen knocking on the sliding door, mouthing es press o.

"Coming, coming, one minute."

"The espresso good?"

"Could be a bit hotter."

"I knocked on the door when it was ready. Do you want me to reheat the coffee? You didn't hear me. I'm not going into that jungle to get eaten up by mosquitoes."

"The coffee is just fine, Helen. It really is."

Helen has done a good job sorting the mail. The windows of the four envelopes from the Trust Department are up and to the left, ready for my review of this month's investment results.

On the days when the trust reports arrived I would explain, discuss the printouts with Dotty. The yeartodate results based on our investment mix of equities and bonds is about what we can expect in this economy.

Dotty, we could have bought a secondtodie insurance policy. When I die and you die, the estate would have taxfree proceeds to pay the taxes. Husbands are supposed to die first, Dotty.

Dotty had died first. Now, if old Fred lives another fifteen years, the trust assets may equal the insurance benefits. The longer Fred lives the more the investment accounts gain on the insurance company results. In twenty years if old Fred is still alive the trust value will exceed the insurance benefits.

In Florida, during the winter holidays when the Sterns gathered in Sanibel, I remember whispering to my daughters This year's trust income was about like last year. Not good, not bad. Emily was the one who understood business. Dad, you enjoy the risk. You always bet on the long shots. You can't stand a sure thing. That's how you run your life.

I am not going to die for at least fourteen more years. Not until the trusts exceed the insurance benefits. Not until Belsky's lease is up! Out you go, Belsky. Sorry, no renewal, nothing to negotiate, no never!

Only Emily was interested in my business affairs. Dad, please send me your yearend reports. All Edna had to say was I am sure you know what you are doing. Edith always asked Are you buying shares in companies that are making a social contribution? I don't want our money invested in polluters and spoilers.

"It's hot out! Fred, you shouldn't be out there breathing that garbage, not with your lungs! Every time you go out, you cough."

"I think I'm allergic to the mold."

"Why don't you find out?"

"Would it matter?"

"Allergies don't go away. You may be getting worse."

"The mold will be gone when it dries out."

"It's supposed to rain tonight."

"You have been watching the weather channel?"

"You were outside so I turned on teevee."

"I don't mind. You know I'm not that observant . . . That was supposed to be a joke."

"Fred, you are not a funny man."

She's right. I know only two humorous stories. Helen has already heard them both. The first, about the doctor who dispensed tranquilizers is awful and my talking dog story is no better.

"I will study my copy of Asimov's Treasury of Humor and prepare myself to be a more entertaining brother."

"Fred, you are limping."

"It's my hip acting up."

"When Dotty was alive and you had a little pain, you ran to the doctor."

"It's only pain. I got used to it."

"So why don't you go to a doctor?"

"I have been."

"You would feel better."

"I can't remember feeling well."

"So . . . ?"

"I take my pills."

"Have you told the doctor how much you hurt?"

"Doctors can only do so much."

"If you weren't living alone . . ."

"My wife would help me on with my socks, tie my shoe laces, massage my cramping legs, prepare my nutritious low salt low cholesterol high fiber kosher meals . . ."

"I am serious, Fred!"

Alex B. Stone

Dotty used to say, Fred, I don't think you could live without a woman to take care of you. You don't even know where the store is. I never answered her. Never even considered life without Dotty. Then Dotty was dead. Suddenly, completely, forever. Dotty and her dissenting opinions gone. Now Emily's gone. Emily knew how hard it was for me those first years after Dotty's death. Call me anytime, Pops.

In a good mood, a jocular mood, Emily would call me Fred. Having trouble with the cleaning woman, Fred? Get four maids in for one hour. You go for a swim, you come home, the maids are gone, the house is clean, the kettle is boiling . . .

Emily was the planner, bought her Exmas ticket to Florida in February, used a United Air Lines Visa chargecard to add to her frequentflyer miles, collected points for her hotel stays, paid her bills on time to deduct the discounts, bought only what she needed. She bought Henri Bendel dresses and Bally shoes at yearend sales and then took her dad to dinner at expensive restaurants where the California Chardonnay was 26 dollars a bottle.

Why don't you save more, Emily? With your income you could save more.

I have a rich father who won't spend a dime on himself, only worries about others.

"I really thought we would have visitors this morning."

"It's that muggy heat, Fred. You don't realize how hot it is. For so early in the day it's awful—and it's not even summer yet. What do you want for lunch?"

"Whatever you like, Helen."

"It's your lunch too, Fred."

"French toast and coffee would be nice."

"You had your espresso, you won't be able to nap."

"Helen, make some decaf."

"That's why you don't sleep. It's all that coffee and eating dry crusts of ryebread before bedtime is not a sleep enhancer either."

All alone in a bedroom built for two with the prints and paintings that Dotty hung. All alone under Dotty's blankets. So cold, I wake up in the middle of the night just frozen. Turn up the heat, Dad. Don't forget to sleep with the nightlight on. Dad, be careful in the shower. You promised to put down the nonslip strips.

I had a grabbar put in. I'm getting ready for the surgery.

You have to decide for yourself, Fred. You understand the risks. It's the groin pain that's so bad.

"You hurt, Fred?"

"I'll go lie down, ease my back. Call me when lunch is ready."

From his bed Fred could see the Matisse etching, a nude portrait of a young woman with dark eyes and the breasts of a yearling goat, could contemplate Emil Carlsen's greyvibrant yet placidly stilllife painting of Pitcher and Quince. On the far wall to the right the 1914 Kirchner drawing of a female nude turned threequarter face to the left. To the left a Miro cat grinned her red eyes as she stalked a fleeing blackandred surreal moth.

On his back, Fred dozed, dreamed his recurrent Kafkadream of gentle terror, something with a trial, witnesses, machinations, Dotty testifying.

Fred awoke, turned on his right side, onto the bad hip, winced, turned to his left side, stretched, arched his back, fell asleep.

The offer to purchase the downtown office building came from a darkskinned, darkeyed man of about thirty wearing a maroon turban, loosewhite cotton shirt over pajamalike deep orange trousers. Beside him his wife, silent, supportive in matching shirt and trousers, carried a child of about six months, dressed as its parents. The child was smiling.

"Lunch!"

"Fred. Why are you grinning?"

"I sold our half empty downtown building."

"You are mad, Fred!"

"I had a vision. An Indian doctor bought the building for an outpatient clinic."

"Your decaf is getting cold."

"I'm right here, Helen.

"Muffins . . . ?"

After lunch, more thankyounotes, then The New York Times. Helen sitting in the Eames chair in the corner with her needle point. Needle in, needle out.

"Fred, you ought to sell the house. It's too big for you, too much for you to take care of."

"The yard does get bigger each year. This year I'm going to hire more done."

"You said that last year."

"I no longer have a choice if I get my hip replaced."

"Reach a decision about something. Decide about something!"

"It doesn't seem important."

"George says you are neglecting your business affairs."

"Business doesn't seem important."

The tradition says you mustn't grieve too much. I'm not going to spend my days in the cemetery. That too is forbidden.

"I'll get things organized. It will take a couple of months."

"You going out again?"

"No, just stretching my back. God, I hurt!"

"You going to lie down?"

"No, I want to get back to my writing."

"I read your last story—Only a Step Behind."

"A Half Step Behind. You liked it?"

"It's about illness and old age."

"That's all I know."

"No wonder you don't get published. What are you working on now?"

"Oh, you won't like that either."

"What is that about?"

"Dying."

"That's beautiful, Fred, just beautiful."

"It is, when your family is all around you." Sitting in a rocker in the gazebo or under the oaks, Edith holding my left hand and Edna, my right. The grandchildren at my feet.

Yes, Papa? Don't say it, Papa.

Chapter Fifteen

"It's Dan Gordon on the phone for you, Fred."

"Too damn hot to play tennis. Can I stop by?"

"Sure!"

"I'll be over in a few minutes."

"Dan Gordon is coming over."

"So?"

"You remember Doctor Gordon, the man with a story for every occasion."

"Sure I do, and his wife Mamie. He is a very charming man."

"He works at it."

"Wouldn't hurt you to try harder. To try to be more pleasant."

"I try."

"Try harder!"

"You sound like . . . something out of Beckett."

"Who?"

"It's not important."

"That's rude, Fred, very rude."

"Okay. Beckett was an Irish French playwright."

"You read too much."

Reading and riting and rithmetic. That's how my evenings progress. Maybe I'm rude because of the pain in my hands or that lousy hungover feeling I wake up with every morning. Maybe it's this or that. Maybe because I am always tired.

"Sorry Helen, I didn't mean to be rude."

"You have enough reason to be edgy—the good Lord knows you do—but you don't have to take it out on me."

"I didn't realize."

"Maybe Doctor Gordon can cheer you up."

"I don't need cheering up."

"I think you are getting depressed."

Helen, the medical maven. Now I am getting depressed. So I am depressed until Monday morning. Then Shiva is over, life begins again. There is a will to be read, the legal requirements of death must be met.

Monday, a day for telephone calls, for leaking hotwaterheaters and leaking roofs.

"Is Doctor Gordon still collecting all those Senior Olympics jogging and swimming medals?"

"Dan is into sports. That is, he's into sports for the last eleven years since he had his bypass."

"You remember dates like that?"

"Dan gives a birthday lunch to celebrate his bypass. He thinks of the bypass surgery as a rebirth."

"Doctor Gordon has just driven up. I think it's Doctor Gordon, in a . . ."

"A white Olds convertible."

"Mamie doesn't seem to be with him."

Dan has a wife that rests every afternoon. Just a little thing she does for herself, like in a Victorian novel.

"You don't have to go to the door, Helen. Dan will let himself in at the side door with a grin and a story."

Dr. Dan Gordon in a red nylon workout suit, azure blue streak sweeping from his shoulders down across his chest to his impressive stomach, presents his teeth in a grin and a tape in his right hand.

"For you, Fred. An inspirational message from Rabbi Blau, my daughter's new age guru."

"I'm not listening to my tape player."

"This is not entertainment, Fred. This is a message for the bereaved, for the grief ridden."

"Fred, I would like to hear what Rabbi Blau has to say about death."

"You ever heard of him, Helen?"

"He's very big in Denver. That's what it says in the insert. So big he gave up his congregation to create these inspirational messages."

"Thank you, Dan. Will you want the tape back?"

"Pass it along to others who may be helped in their life crisis by Rabbi Blau's message."

"I get my crises resolved at morning prayers."

"Fred is the lucky one. All that faith while I am still searching."

"Listen to the tape, Helen, it could help."

"That's what gurus are for."

"What's new at the hospital?"

Dan sits in the rocker, feet flat on the floor, begins to rock. "Dancing with the HMOs, Fred, dancing with the insurance companies. And it's the patient who gets his toes stepped on. Not like in the old days. Insurance companies playing God!"

"That must hurt!"

"Things don't change for the better, Fred."

"What have you been doing with yourself Dan?"

"Practicing. Senior Olympics coming up . . . Did you hear the one about the fellow from Rockville who went to New York City to hear Perlman play his fiddle? He starts out from his hotel, gets just a little lost. He sees a distinguished looking elderly man carrying a violin case. Surely he would know the way to Carnegie Hall. Excuse me, I am a stranger in town. Can you please tell me how do I get to

If I Could Sleep . . .

Carnegie Hall?"

Dan screws up his face, makes his voice old and wise.

"Practice, young man, practice!"

Dan laughs. Helen grins, Fred grins.

"It's an oldie, but you tell it well."

"Thank you, Fred—it's hard to find one he hasn't heard at his age. He knows too much! Your brother is my resource for all things Hebrew, Yiddish and French. I call Fred for all the answers."

"Dan does crossword puzzles."

"Fred is never wrong."

Fred Stern, full of booklearning, overeducated and underutilized. Heard all the jokes, too.

Just can't tell them.

"I baked some muffins earlier. Let me bring them out."

"They're low fat, low cholesterol. Bran, you know. Helen is very health conscious."

"It's wonderful to have a sister like that. I can see she cares about you a great deal. Say, Fred, did you hear the one about the young woman goes to the baker's orders two dozen muffins?"

"No, Dan, but something tells me you should save that one for the locker room."

"There, gentlemen! Dr. Gordon, will you have tea or coffee?"

"Please! Call me Dan."

"Well, Dan, did you ever try to talk some sense into Fred about not living alone?"

"Helen wants me to open a literary and art beeanbee to show off my art collection, my library and my culinary skills."

"My brother is losing his mind. He thinks that is funny."

"For someone that stubborn, Fred's head is about a good as you are going to get in Rockville."

"Thank you, Doctor. Helen wants me to stalk a young widow, bring her back alive to Rockville. To manage me and my empire."

Alex B. Stone

"That's not that bad an idea, Fred. Actually, you know, Mamie has a friend who was in her class at Syracuse. Her husband just died."

Helen pricks her ears. "Where is she living?"

"Milwaukee. Mamie could invite her down for a weekend. We could all go out to dinner at La Tosca. You like French food, don't you, Fred?"

"As long as I can bring an interpreter."

"Just talk to her, Fred. What harm would that do? What is her name?"

"Laura. Oh. These muffins are exceptional!"

"That's a nice name. Fred?"

Find Fred a significant other. Better yet, get him married. My brother Fred the widower. The poor man lives all alone, thinks he can manage. You ought to see his clothes. He hasn't bought a suit since his wife died and that is almost ten years. Everything he puts on is either too tight or completely out of style. George wouldn't garden in the clothes my brother wears to his office. A man of his means walking around with buttons off his jackets, his ties creased! Whenever I visit Rockville, all I do is sew on buttons, fix the hems on his slacks, let out his trousers. I let out trousers he bought at Harrod's on his first trip to England in 1959!

"I agree with you, Helen. It isn't good for Fred to be alone."

"You hear, Fred?

First thing Laura would do is walk into our bedroom—because that is going to be our bedroom—Is that a bronze statue of a cow on your dresser? Yes, it is. That is the work of Leon Bonheur, one of the great French animal sculptors. Why is her tail up and her neck extended? That, Laura, is a cow in heat, in estrus, longing, bellowing for her bull to come to her, to service her, to satisfy her, to fulfill her desire. Don't talk dirty, Fred. That's not dirty, that's . . . My God, Fred, all those nude pictures! Fred, really, do you think they belong in our bedroom? The Lester Johnson Walking Women in their tootight

141

dripdry summer dresses. You have so many lovely landscapes and seascapes, Fred. I am sure we can find two or three others that we will both enjoy looking at. You won't mind if I hang the nudes in your den. It's not a den, Laura, it's a library. Finest art library between Chicago and Des Moines. Have you actually read all those books?

"You are a good looking man, Fred. You don't have to spend the rest of your life alone."

"Laura would want my moustache off."

"What did you say, Fred?"

"I said that your bran muffins are excellent."

"You said something about Laura."

"It was nothing."

The enigma of tomorrow. I have enough problems managing today. Now I have to take on tomorrow with Laura. We will talk of my aspirations, her plans for our new lives together, expose our selves, to know each other better.

Philip Guston. Early 'Seventies. Cartoonlike oils. Painted himself as a hooded figure. Face covered to hide the pain of his struggle, the anxieties of his creative process. In his right hand his brushes, in his left a cigarette burned to a stub. He watched the canvas come to life on his easel through the slits in his hood.

Fred, let's take the Kluxton out of the dining room. I think the Kluxton painting would look better in your library . . .

"Fred, would you like for me to tell Mamie about Laura?"

"Please, Helen."

"Dotty has been dead for almost ten years."

"And Emily?"

"Emily wouldn't want you to be alone."

"You could join us for dinner with Laura. I am sure Laura is not after your fortune. She has more than enough of her own. She's an attractive gal, Fred."

"Does she have children?"

Alex B. Stone

"All grown. The oldest son a doctor, a daughter a lawyer, the youngest is gay but has sworn to his mother to use condoms. Each one a smiling achiever. The gay one is a commodity broker in Chicago with a weekend hideaway condo—piedaterre—in San Francisco. Laura will be going to Sarasota for the winter. If you hit it off with her you could invite her down to Sanibel to meet Edith and Edna."

Dad, it's really all right for you to live in sin. You really don't have to get married at your age.

Her place my place, her condo my condo, her bank account my bank account, her children my children, her paintings my paintings, all described in a prenuptial agreement and kept current with a yearly codicil to my will her will.

"If you like, I'll give Mamie the word. You know how efficient she is. She just loves to plan."

Say yes and before Laura materializes for her weekend with the Gordons Mamie will call me six times. Warnings, admonitions, suggestions. Fred, you should buy a new suit. Fred, if Laura talks about her grandchildren (you know how women are) please be tolerant. None of your cynical comments and please Fred unless you absolutely must don't come in on your black cane. Carry your handcarved in Haiti. It's more playful. And please Fred don't tell about your arthritis. Everyone hurts. Fred don't tell a humorous story. Dan will take care of that. Fred, why don't you come by before we go to dinner? We can all go in one car. Dan will open a bottle of champagne. Laura loves Asti Spumante.

Asti Spumante. Sweet Italian piss! I'll bring a bottle of Made in America Korbel Brut!

Helen is plotzing. Dan sees it too.

"Now, Helen, let's not push him. Now is not the time. Mamie will call Fred in a couple of days. Fred, do you want to come over next Friday for dinner?"

"I don't know . . ."

"It would do you good."

What kind of Sabbath dinner is it at the Gordons' when Mamie doesn't light candles, Dan doesn't break Challah, do the blessings over the wine?

"Fred, you remember the power of attorney for health that you gave me? The one in which you named Emily, well . . . ?"

"I know. I understand."

"At our age one shouldn't be without a health power of attorney."

No powerofattorney down goes the trachea tube, on goes the breathingmachine, in goes the needle. No more powerofattorney. Henceforth the good Lord will decide when I die. No ghoulish discussions about pulling the plug on dear old dad. Or give Laura the powerofattorney. Let Laura share in the joys of a second marriage.

Really Fred, you should sell some of your paintings. No one can see them stacked up along the wall. Let's sell them and use the money for something useful.

You are right, Laura. We'll hold a lawn sale. Or I'll donate the paintings to the museum, take them off as a taxsaving gift. The catch is, first you have to have a tax obligation. Sell at auction. No matter the price you get you will have a tax obligation. Sell out, Fred, let's go places and do things. Cruise with the Cunard Line. Thirty percent reduction on this fall's cruises to the MiddleEast from Athens to Haifa. First person pays full fare, second person pays half. Single rooms reserved at 125% of the first passenger fare. Twentyfive percent more to travel without a Sancho. Peace and tranquility at only one fourth more . . .

"Fred, I'll be going now."

"Thank you for coming, Dan."

"Great muffins, Helen. Thank you."

"Low fat, low salt, high fiber."

"The virtues of home baking."

"Good bye, Fred. I'll call you in a few days."

"I have never seen anyone eat a muffin like you do, Fred. No one eats the top first and then crumbles the rest with their fingers. You got crumbs all over the rug."

"I'll vacuum it up."

"No, I'll do it. You take the tray into the kitchen."

Emily would go off to her group on Friday afternoons. Afterwards sometimes she would call just to talk. How is it going, Pops? Dad, what are you going to do on the weekend? You ought to go out more, Pops.

I'll drive over to Iowa City. The University Art Museum has an exhibit of French Symbolist paintings—mostly Eugène Carrière.

Mostly the prints you gave them, Pops.

How is the practice going?

Fine, Pops, just fine. Pops, you want to come to Denver for Thanksgiving?

No more trips to Denver. No more Emily and her dogood projects. When Emily was ten she staged a neighborhood magic show. Only ten cents to fight muscular dystrophy.

Pops, go out for a walk. Put up your hammock. You haven't put it up in ten years. Lay on your back, watch the clouds go by.

Don't get too busy, Emily. Save a little time for yourself. When my daughters were little, I was too busy. Too busy.

Emily, did you have a happy childhood?

I don't remember being unhappy.

Don't you remember the poisonpen letters you wrote? When you were about twelve, thirteen, you used to throw the letters down into the living room. Mama, Papa, I hate you!

I don't remember. I don't think of my childhood as being unhappy.

If I Could Sleep . . .

I was talking to Alice—she's an architect—I want you to meet her—I met her in group—she has become a special friend of mine—Alice and I were talking about growing up. Alice asked me the very same question about growing up with sisters.

I didn't know you were in a therapy group.

Just a women's support group, Pops. Exploring ourselves. Going back, back into the womb for happiness through insight.

Happy is he whose help is the God of Jacob, whose hope is in the Lord.

"Go take a nap, Fred. Your eyes are shutting. I don't want you falling asleep if anyone else comes."

"I think it's the half of your sleep aid that you gave me. I have been feeling stupid all day."

"You can't get that from half a pill. There is a florist's delivery van in the drive."

"It's my order."

"Go rest."

"That's all I do is rest."

"You can't keep your eyes open."

"I'll lie down and read."

"Try to fall asleep."

"You'll wake me if anyone comes!"

"Are you expecting anyone in particular?

"I thought Herman Gottwalt would surely come."

"Is he still the Rabbi's right hand man?"

"Keeps him busy. He teaches the converts."

"Don't talk so much. Go rest."

"You'll be leaving Sunday. Helen, if I forget . . . I want to thank you."

"Don't thank me. Go rest!"

Alex B. Stone

"You could rest too, Helen."

"I have the chicken to get ready."

Tradition, tradition. Chicken on Friday night. Cold breakfast and cold lunch on Saturday. We don't light the stove on Saturday but it's all right to turn on the heat. Dad, does that make sense?

No, not really Emily. It's just easier not to cook.

Helen may not even be aware that she is performing deeds of lovingkindness for the living and dead. She accompanied Emily to her grave, she helped with the meal of consolation, she stayed for the Shiva. That, Helen, is our tradition.

"Helen, I want to thank you."

"For what?"

"You made it easier for me. This was not a time for me to be alone."

"You shouldn't be alone."

"I know Dotty wouldn't want me to be alone. That's what my daughters said. We are sure Mama wouldn't want you to be alone in her double bed.

Turn on the readinglight. Middle Passage by Charles Johnson. Ten minutes. Shut the book shut the light desperately seek sleep.

Chapter Sixteen

"Fred, you were talking. Were you calling me?"

"Dreams, Helen."

"Bad dreams?"

"Memories."

Emily fourteen. Our week of vacation on a dude ranch in the San Juan forest of southwest Colorado. Casting for trout in a stream so clear you can see the speckles as they take the hook. Dotty on the cabin porch, reading. Fred, you go riding with the girls. I'll have my lunch in the dining room. The trailride was to end with a chuckwagon cookout beside a glacial lake.

From the ranch the trail ascended slowly, easily. The horses in file walked carefully on the rock outcroppings. The sun rose above the mountain peak to dry the native grass. About ten we stopped in a meadow from which the first hay had been cut, took off our sweaters. From there the trail began its descent into the bowl that contained the lake. The horses set their legs to control their slide into the little valley. I sat back in the saddle, braced to keep my horse in line behind the girls. Emily was first down onto the flat, behind her, Edith, Edna.

The horses began to gallop. Perhaps it was their thirst for the water, or they knew the sooner they reached the lake the sooner they would be free of their riders or maybe they were just as hungry as we were. Those last few galloping minutes were like the cavalry charge in a John Wayne movie. Side by side our horses raced towards the lake. The girls laughed, screamed. Myself, sweating, frightened that my horse would stumble, throw me to the ground. It was my fear first, then the fear for my daughters' safety.

When we got to the lake, Emily dismounted, caught the bridle of my mount, held it while I extricated myself from the sweated horn of the western saddle.

You done good, Pops! I didn't think you would stay on.

My legs were shaking. Haven't been on a horse in twenty years. Now I know why!

You done good, Pops.

It was that year or the next that the girls gave up horses—that is until Emily went to veterinary school.

"You are all sweaty, Fred."

"We were racing, the girls and I, riding towards a lake. Those dreams—replays, ancient memories, lost and forgotten. Helen. I hadn't thought of that week in Colorado until just now. Here it is, almost thirty years later and it all comes back."

"That's because of Emily."

"In my dream I was frightened, my heart bouncing, thumping. Afraid I would get hurt or killed. I was concerned about me, only me—not about Emily or Edna or Edith . . ."

"You should have nothing but good memories of Emily. She was a very caring daughter. She worried about you. Whenever Emily called me we always talked about you, about your being alone. Emily was always amazed how well you were doing."

"Emily called every weekend."

Where have you been, Pops? Running after the girls? Pops, you don't have to send me checks. The practice is going very well. You have done enough for me.

If I send to Edith and Edna, I send to you.

Pops, what made you leave economics?

Alex B. Stone

I guess it was the challenge. Theory was too easy. Wanted to get my hands on something solid, lasting, real. I wanted to be able to see the fruit of my work, show it to others, effect changes in people's lives for the better. I guess I wanted to emulate Papa somehow. You know, he was just a oneman country practice. Calving in the spring, hogs to vaccinate against cholera and erysipelas. Herd testing of cattle for tuberculosis and brucellosis. Strip down to his underpants to birth those cows.

Did construction fulfill that in you?

I complained about the relentless pace of the work. Not enough time for myself, for Dotty, for my girls. But I think I enjoyed the work. That is, until I became arthritic. Then, when the slump hit us, it seemed like a good moment to shut it down.

Is that when you began writing?

I always kept a journal. I am proud of you, Emily, for asking that. Why, Pops?

How is your love life, Pops?

I've been offered the romantic lead in a B movie. I'm off to Hollywood in six weeks.

Pops, you are out of your mind!

Have to stay cheerful and optimistic. I hold to the stubborn belief, unfounded in experience, contrary to wisdom, that tomorrow will be better, will bring me a bit of success in business, a bit of recognition for my writing. Else how could I get up in the morning, invest another day, another halfpint of blood into my work?

Dad, you are a success. You created the life you wanted, married the woman you loved. You built good, solid housing, made a fortune.

And lost it . . .

You publish your short stories.

Sure. A regular Somerset Maugham . . .

If I Could Sleep . . .

"Get up, Fred, you'll feel better. It's quit raining, you could go out in the yard, sit in the sun."

Summer before spring. The mildew is growing on the concrete, climbing up the board and batten to the second floor.

"It's almost time to get ready for the Sabbath."

"Plenty of time, Fred. Go out. Go for a walk."

"I'll go for a walk on the Sabbath, Helen."

No mourning on the Sabbath.

Emily and me, off for a summer week in the Minnesota Boundarywaters with its smell of the pine woods. A fragrance that doesn't travel south into the Mississippi River Valley of northern Illinois. Just father and daughter in an aluminum canoe. She was fifteen, as tall and strong as she was ever to be. Emily had planned the trip, made the arrangements with the outfitter. I'll cook, Pops. All you have to do is sit in the back and paddle. Didn't tell me about the portage to the lake with the island where we were to camp. Eightyfive pounds of canoe on my back, the paddles in my hand, Emily toting the food, tent and essentials packs.

At sunset the moose stood in the lake to graze along the shore. The quiet sunsets. I remember that dawn and the early mornings and the midday storm that swept across the lake.

Pops, let's paddle across the lake, look at the waterfall.

Emily with map in the bow of the canoe, gloved hands and arms paddling a steady rhythm. The wind shifted, rose, waves slapped the aluminum sides, began to break over the gunwale. The trapped water chilled our feet, rose in the canoe bottom.

Emily changed course, headed the canoe into the wind. The waves broke now over the bow. Emily wet and triumphant when we beached at the campground.

It was worth it, wasn't it, Pops?

More excitement than I needed.

Beautiful waterfall.

Too dangerous for me, Emmy. I thought we were going to tip. We were a long way from shore.

I would have saved you, Pops.

"Helen, do you know that I still have Emily's Girl Scout merit badges?"

"It's no sense talking to you, Fred. You don't hear me."

"I hear you."

"So...?"

"I promise I'll call Mamie. I promise I'll go to dinner with Laura. I promise."

"It's for your own good Fred. You can't go on your way."

"I'll buy a new suit to make a good impression on Laura."

"It won't do you a bit of harm to be civil to her. Laura may be ..."

"The woman of my dreams. I'm not up to dating. What do I do, take Laura to the Dairy Queen for a low fat yogurt with NutraSweet?"

"You could take her for a cruise on the President. It's not every city that has a gambling boat."

Laura is beautiful, trim, observant. She doesn't ride on the Sabbath—or gamble. Laura laughs at my attempts at humor, but Laura does not read my short stories. Fred, you are amazing! To think of all those careers you've had! A businessman who writes! You have written a play? How unusual! A published author who still goes downtown every morning. Such a lovely oldfashioned Sabbath service. Beautiful synagogue. How can Rockville with so small a congregation afford such a beautiful synagogue?

Debt and bingo.

I don't know if I could live in Rockville, Fred. Mamie tells me you have a condo in Florida. Sanibel?

Would you like to see the treefarm?

I didn't bring hiking shoes.

Those shoes are fine. That's red clover. The farmhouse was down the lane. The barn was to the left. There was a red machineshed with an aluminum roof. Beside it was a white chickenhouse leanto.

What happened to the buildings?

They were vandalized. The red barnboards could be panelling for a basement recreation room.

Laura slips her hand into mine.

Fred, have you ever been to the Orient?

Korea. I flew a B-29 in the war. Plane burned. Lungs damaged by smoke.

Laura's eyes well up, gaze deeply into mine.

The air in Bali is so intoxicating! Very romantic . . .

Not now, Laura. Maybe after the surgery. Now I am fully scheduled. Dermatologist on Tuesday, dentist on Thursday, then to the internist who will order an EKG and chestplates. Necessary precautions, Mr. Stern, before your hip replacement. Next, the anesthesiologist. I would prefer a spinal anesthetic. That's wise, Mr. Stern. Especially with your vacuolated left lung. Are you coughing, Mr. Stern?

My internist says the cough is due to the antihypertensive drugs that I take morning and night.

"What are you writing, Fred?"

"A note to myself to cancel my doctor's appointment on Monday."

"Maybe you ought to go."

"It's only to arrange for my autologous blood collection. I can wait until forty days before the surgery to begin collecting."

"That would give you only three or four days before your first donation."

"Thursday would be better than Monday."

"You okay, Fred?"

"I took two Tylenol. I don't feel well when I can't sit in the whirlpool, when I don't swim."

"You could take a hot bath."

"I'll see. It's so hard for me to get in and out of that bath tub."

"I could help you."

"We'll see."

"There are mechanical lifter uppers and putter downers that fit into baths."

"I'll have to get one."

"When?"

"I'll have to get around to that. I can't put that off. When I come home, after the surgery."

"You put everything off."

"Not everything."

"For example!"

"I pay my taxes on time."

"Go out for a walk, Fred. When you come back, you can open the Chardonnay. I'll take out the Challah from the freezer. Mrs. Katz makes a beautiful Challah. Go already! I'll set the table, prepare the candles."

"Plenty of time, Helen. Candle lighting isn't until six thirty six."

"Will you look at that! It's raining again."

"I'll go out anyway. Just in the yard, though."

"You don't have to announce what you are going to do, Fred, just do it."

"I have to order some potting soil."

"It's too wet to plant, you said so yourself."

"For the pots of impatiens."

"Go already! I want to call George and you're distracting me."

"Tell him I'm keeping you here in Rockville. I'm granting him visitation rights."

"George needs me too, Fred."

"Of course he needs you. Go, call him."

If I Could Sleep . . .

I need you, too, Helen. I need Emily, Dotty, Edith, Edna, a good night's sleep.

"What are you mumbling, Fred?"

"I said I'm looking forward to Sabbath morning prayers."

"You can pray at home."

"Prayer is community."

"In your congregation, Fred, you are a community praying for its dead. Without the dead you wouldn't have a minyan."

"Death keeps us alive, Helen."

Chapter Seventeen

"Fred, do you want me to call Herman, tell him you are expecting him?"

"No, if he could he would be here. Herman is very good about fulfilling the commandment of visiting the mourners."

"Maybe he put it off until tomorrow."

"I doubt it. Herman would know not to make a condolence call on the Sabbath."

"You okay, Fred? You are grimacing."

"I don't feel so well."

"You hungry?"

"No, it's my back."

"You could have gone for your massage."

You are right, Helen. You are always right.

"How was I to know I would hurt until it happened?"

You have enough experience Fred. You just won't learn. You are the slowest man to learn.

Yes, Dotty.

"Do you want me to set the table?"

"Sit, read your paper."

"Did you see yesterday's New York Times where a HUD official was found guilty of accepting bribes?"

Bribery one thing I did not stoop to. Well, only once. It was only twothousand dollars to a citycouncilman to resolve a zoning question. The outcome was for the common good so it was not really a bribe. More like a political contribution.

In Rockville we have a real need for public leadership. Our city staffers still permit leafburning which is an abomination to man and beast. Every fall asthmatic children wheeze out their protests before the City Council: Ban Leaf Burning!

Rockville Seeks Gambling License for Riverboat Operator.

Illinois from city to county to state overtaxed overregulated over-burdened. Mostly untalented if not wholly inept political types run the show.

Rockville blessed with two congregations. One Conservative, one Reform. Bat Yam, my congregation in Florida, Reform with strong underpinnings of conservatism. I belong to all three. Our rabbis offer adult education, ranging from Hebrew reading to mysticism. We are fortunate to have an annual Judaic lecture at Rockville College. That's the Stern Lectures, of course. The subjects have ranged from Biblical archeology to Israel in the twentyfirst century.

"Fred, will you open the wine?"

"In a while, Helen."

"The burgundy has to breathe."

"It can hold its breath for another hour or two—it's only three thirty."

"What are you reading?"

"The Fast Forward Page."

"What is that?"

"It's about café life on the Upper West Side of New York City. You ever been to Café Lalo, two o one West Eightythird Street?"

"Fred, you know we live in the East Side. No wonder you don't get anything done, wasting your life reading about Café Lalo. When would you go to Café Lalo? When were you in New York last?"

"Helen, am I a man of high ethical values?"

"Fred, you are mad."

"No, really, Helen. Am I?"

"I would suppose so with all your praying."

"Praying has nothing to do with ethics."

"Okay, Fred. You are a man of high ethical values. That please you? If that is what you need, you are a man of rare and sterling qualities."

That was not what Dotty said. Dotty said Fred you are getting greedy. Greedy!

"Helen, you know I wrote to Emily every week?"

"What could you write every week?"

"Business things, and about how things were going with me and the world. Did Emily write to you?"

"She sent me cute postcards when she travelled. Emily had a very sly sense of humor."

Emily sent me cards too. Emily and I had long intimate visits on the telephone. Evidently It was easier for Emily not to talk to me facetoface. We hardly talked at all when she came to Florida, but on the telephone we spoke about everything.

Dad, were you and Mom happy?

We were not unhappy. That is, I was not unhappy with your mother. Whether your mother was happy, that is another matter. Your mother wanted a more perfect world—more perfect each day.

Fred, why are your utility bills so high? Fred, why are our maintenance people having so many problems with our heating system? Fred, do you know what these inefficiencies are costing you?

I know, Dotty, but what can I do about it? Rates go up, one winter is colder than another, the equipment is old. Call IowaIllinois GasandElectric, get an efficiency expert in here.

That's what things cost, Mr. Stern. I understand your building is half empty, but . . .

Thank you. It was very good of the powercompany to review my bills. That's what things cost, Dotty. We are about as efficient as a halfempty building can be.

You don't pay the business any attention, Fred. You are more involved in your prayers, in your writing, in your charities. Fred, until I come down here you don't know what is going on in your own business. Ethel signs the checks. Do you ever look at the checks?

How would looking at the powercompany checks change how much we owe for gasandelectricity and utility taxes and utility delivery charges and efficiency charges?

Fred, complain to the State Utility Commission.

You complain to the Utility Commission, Dotty. I don't enjoy fighting City Hall.

If you would pay attention to your business, Fred.

Okay, I'll pay attention.

Who is happy, Emily? The Sages of the Mishna answer: He who is satisfied with his portion.

"I don't think anyone will be coming this afternoon, Fred, if you want to set the table. You want me to help you up?"

"I think you will have to. My knees are swollen stiff."

"You should have gone swimming."

"It's the last day of Shiva for Emily."

"Fred, you don't have to jump up to clear the table the minute you finish eating. The dishes can wait."

"It does me good to get up."

"Leave the tea and Challah . . . Fred, while you are up, would you get me some of the Chambord strawberry jam that I brought? It's in the pantry, next to the olive oil. And bring a clean plate for yourself. The Challah is delicious. That is one thing I can't buy in New York. Homemade Challah."

"I had enough, Helen. I usually don't eat that much chicken soup. And chicken. And pears in wine sauce for dessert! You're spoiling me, Helen."

"It's not wine, Fred, it's Puerto Rican rum."

"It's rum?"

"Yes, rum."

Helen has dessert with breakfast, lunch and dinner. She covers her bulk with a sack, wears dresses designed by Marina of Milan. For the fuller uppermiddleclass mature figure.

Poor Dotty gave up desserts candy cookies ice cream. She still gained weight. Maybe it was because she had a touch of diabetes. It was only a sugar intolerance. Dr. Hellman warned Dotty. Mrs. Stern, so far you have been fortunate. Diabetes is an insidious disease which can damage your kidneys, affect your nerves, impair your vision. Come back in three months. I would like another look at your retinas. Mrs. Stern, no sweets, no sugars, no cheating. It may be best you tell your daughters. Their physician should be aware of your being a diabetic.

Dotty had told me at Thanksgiving dinner, after eating only a halfportion of her pumpkin pie. I have to cut back on my sugar intake. You know Grandma was diabetic. My mother died from kidney failure, but that was before we had dialysis. No, I don't have to take insulin.

Did Dr. Hellman check your eyes?

Emily, quit worrying. Everything is fine.

Mother, you could . . .

Don't mother me, Emily. Would you like some cherry pie? I made it especially for you.

Dotty, what did Dr. Hellman say?

Dr. Hellman thinks I should see a retinal specialist.

No autopsy, Dr. Hellman. Our religion prohibits unnecessary mutilation.

Only a small section of the back of the left eye would be disturbed. You would not notice any change. The examination of the retinal blood vessels would determine if there had been a hemorrhage.

Why the left eye, Dr. Hellman?

On her last exam, Mrs. Stern had signs of retinal vascular changes. Retinal hemorrhage is a possibility.

Mrs. Stern may have been mildly diabetic, but she died of the trauma. There is no need for an autopsy.

I have to replace my powerofattorney with instructions to Edith not to permit an autopsy on the body of Fred B. Stern. The human body is made in the Lord's image. Must be treated with respect, returned to the earth intact if possible. Your body is a loaner, Fred B. Stern.

"Thank you, Helen, it was a fine supper. Beats my heat and serve Sabbath for one meal.

"You could go . . ."

"I could go to restaurants. I don't like restaurants."

"Fred, all I was going to say is you do have choices. After all, you do have friends. You know, Fred, I was thinking I could stay until Tuesday if you like. George can get along for another few days without me. He doesn't mind eating at his club."

An act of lovingkindness. You bought a stayoversaturday reducedrate roundtrip airfare and were embarrassed to mention it. Why the charade, Helen?

"That would be nice, Helen."

"Show some enthusiasm, Fred. Aren't you pleased that I'm staying?"

"You know I am."

"You could say so."

"Helen, if I said everything I'm feeling . . ."

Alex B. Stone

Dotty, how I miss you. I love you, kiss me, tell me you love me, Dotty. I must have some redeeming qualities . . .

Fred, you forgot to put the jam in the refrigerator! Fred, why did you get up without taking the serving plates? I went to get the tray. You could have taken a couple of dishes. So what if I walk the thirty feet from the dining room into the kitchen empty handed? Fred, that tray is too heavy for you with your back. It's okay, Dotty. It's not okay, Fred. Look at yourself. You are walking all bent over. It's my back. When you get up, wait before you start walking and then you will walk straighter.

"It's very thoughtful of you to stay, Helen. It really is, I appreciate it. Just your answering the telephone is a Godsend to me. I can't handle the condolence calls."

I just heard about Emily. Fred, I am truly sorry. If there is anything I can do, call me. I will. It is good of you to call. Your calling does help . . .

Every morning eleven o'clock I called Dotty from my office. Hello, lover! Who? Me, Fred! Your husband!

Emily called on Saturdays or Sundays. When Dotty was alive, Emily called any day of the week. Sometimes twice a day. Mom, I need your kugel recipe. Where is Dad?

Burning the oak leaves.

Don't let him breathe that crud.

Fred, put on a coat if you are going out, it's raining again.

The rainsounds, the oaktwigs that scrape, scratch, crawl across the shedroof awaken me. Dotty is breathing heavily—so heavily I turn so we are not face to face. Try to fall asleep, it's only two in the morning on what will be a sunny spring day.

❦

"What are you writing, Fred?"

"Just a note to myself to have the gutters cleaned out. The downspouts must be clogged, the rain is dripping off the roof."

"I don't know how you can live here, Fred. With your arthritis you should try Arizona."

"It's my fibromyalgia that is the worst. Isn't anything can be done for that."

"You haven't tried."

"Next week you could go to Arizona, take off for a week or two. What harm will that do?"

"You are right, Helen."

"I know you. You won't do a damn thing."

"I have Emily's affairs."

"Okay, go to Denver for a few days, then go on to Arizona. If I can help you with anything, you know I will."

Helen. You want to see Emily's will. I would bet there is nothing in there for you and yours. Nothing very much anyway. The best you can hope for is that Emily left you her recipe books.

"You going to turn on McNeal Lehrer?"

"No, not tonight. It's the Sabbath."

"It's only the news. Why don't you taste the jam, Fred? You can't buy French jam in Rockville. Try it. You will like it."

No French jam in Rockville. No Woody Allen movies, no heavy traffic. Mostly petty crime.

"It's very good."

"Put more jam on the bread; that's not enough jam."

"It's enough."

"I could heat up the tea."

"It's warm enough, it really is."

"You want to call Edith or Edna?"

"What shall I tell them?"

"They worry about you."

"They know you are here."

"When are you going to Denver?"

"I'll see. I've got to take care of the roof downtown."

"The sooner you sell it, the more you will get."

Get for whom? I don't need it. Edith and Edna don't need. Helen and George don't need. Thank God we don't need!

"That's true."

"Emily had some paintings?"

"Mostly prints. Emily had very good taste."

"You say that because you liked what she bought."

Dad, I think I should buy artworks by women.

Living or dead?

Be serious, Dad. I am asking your advice.

Buy the best. Buy what you like.

Whose work shall I look at? You know the modernists—tell me.

Marguerite Zorach, who began as a lace designer. She did wonderful landscapes, red barns on the brown New England hills. Isabel Bishop, a great draftsman. Shall I say, draftswoman? Her drawings are mostly unappreciated. Everyone knows her prints of the working girls, but her drawings are more personal statements, not so handsome. Look for the drawings, and don't forget Kay Sage, a surrealist. She was a rare bird in the American art scene. A female surrealist with a vision all her own. Look. Enjoy. And try to find a Florine Stetheimer. I don't think they can be bought, but finding and looking are fun too.

"Emily had some great prints. I remember a Marini and a Miro and that Guston of a car that is right out of the cartoons."

"Sounds like your work, Fred. Did you buy them for Emily?"

"No."

"What are you going to do with her art collection?"

"I don't know. I'll wait and see. Maybe there are instructions in Emily's will."

If I Could Sleep . . .

"You know what is in that will."

"I don't know."

"You won't tell me."

"I forget, Helen. Some things I forget."

"You don't forget business things. Not anything to do with a dollar."

Dotty was beginning to forget things. Not in any way that really affected our lives, just in little ways. Dotty made cranberry sauce and forgot to serve it. Dotty bought blankets and more blankets and more blankets.

I'll return them, Fred. I forgot I had blankets in the dressingroom drawers.

Drawers I designed specifically for blankets.

You know what happened this morning at the Book Club?

What, Dotty?

I forgot the name of the book and the author.

Did you remember the plot?

Yes, I did.

Dotty, shut off the TV. We have seen that old flick at least twice.

So you see an old movie a couple of times. What is the big deal? I don't know how you can remember those old movies.

Don't worry about it, Dotty.

Dotty's forgetfulness has nothing to do with her driving across the doubleyellow line headon into an oncoming truck.

What? Mrs. Stern depressed? Had she talked of suicide?

Not to me. There were absolutely no changes in Dorothy's behavior patterns.

Your mother was on her way home from the airport. The late afternoon sun dazzled, confused her. Mother was totally unaware that she had crossed into the oncoming lane.

Why would mother choose to pass a cement truck in a clearly marked No Passing zone?

Your mother didn't see the nopass sign.

On a road she has driven for thirty years?

That is all. It was an accident. Accidents happen every day. Fortyfive thousand people a year die in autoaccidents.

"Helen, I am going to turn up the air conditioner, make it a little warmer. Seventy is too cold for an old arthritic."

"Why don't you get a sweater?"

"I get chilled all over."

"It's the rain. It has rained every day this week."

"Mostly through the nights."

"Be technical, Fred. It's still damp!"

"It was hot this morning!"

The sun was shining as we buried Emily, glints off the stained varnished polished wooden box. No water in the open grave. Mine the first shovel of loose soil to cover the coffin of my firstborn. Together the Rabbi and I and Edith and Edna recited the Kaddish. May there be abundant peace from heaven and life for us and for all Israel and say Amen. May He Who establishes peace in the Heavens grant peace unto us and unto all Israel and say ye Amen.

"It's raining again, don't go out."

"I'll open the front door. I want to have a look."

"You were just outside!"

Every morning we pray for rain. Love the Lord your God, and serve Him with all your heart and with all your soul and I will give rain for your land in its season, the early rain and the late rain, that you may gather in your grain, your wine and your oil.

Lord, our spring rain is more than sufficient. Dear God, it's time for You to dry the land with sun and wind so that we may plant our grain.

"Why are you grinning?"

If I Could Sleep . . .

"I just thought of something."

"What's so funny?"

"Every morning we pray for rain."

"So pray to have it stop raining."

"That's very good, Helen, very good. Helen, do you have to do needle work on Friday night?"

"It's not work. Some do crosswords. You read, you write on the Sabbath."

"You are right, Helen, absolutely right. I shouldn't have said that."

"Fred, don't get up."

"I'll answer the phone.

"It's Herman Gottwalt. He wants to know if you want him to pick you up tomorrow morning to go to services."

"Tell him thank you, that would be very nice of him."

There is always someone worse off than you are. There is nothing that can't be rationalized. Not the death of your wife, not the death of your daughter. Herman is worse off than I am. Leah took her half of the business and ran off to live the life of an aging lesbian with Jennie McCall. Then Jennie studies, converts. Now, once or twice a week Jennie shows up at services, where Herman can pray together with his replacement. Then, on the Sabbath, right there, in the left center where he and Leah used to sit as a family—Jennie McCall sitting beside Leah and the grandchildren!

"How is Herman making it? I mean his being alone."

"Has he got a choice?"

"Herman has a choice. He can remarry."

"You tell him when he stops by to pick me up."

Chapter Eighteen

"Thank you, Herman, for picking me up."

"No trouble, Fred."

"Anything new?"

"The same old thing, Fred. Nothing changes in Rockville. Did you see a new face at services?"

"Just us chickens. We are lucky if we have thirty on Shabbos."

"Do you mind if I stop for gas?"

"Be my guest."

"Fred, open up the glove compartment door, release the gas cap for me, will you?"

"Sure. Your back hurt, Herman?"

"My back, my this, my that. Mostly my angina."

"You taking your nitro?"

"I walk in the mall, I take my nitro and I hurt."

Herman waits for a gas pump to free up that will let him exit west and then make a right turn north into the only street that takes me home. Herman is becoming very cautious.

"Herman, it's cold out there, let me pump the gas for you."

"If you don't mind, Fred. I really don't feel so well."

"What's the matter?"

"Just tired."

If I Could Sleep . . .

"You have a bad night?"

"Not a good one. How is your hip, Fred?"

"I have to use a cane if I am going for a walk—that is, for any distance."

"You didn't take your cane."

"I don't need it for in and out of the car."

Getting gas with you, Fred, is a regular adventure. Why do you wait in line? You could have gone right onto the other island.

I would have been facing the wrong way to go home.

You could back up, Fred.

I don't really see all that well behind me. I can't turn my neck.

Now you have to get the car washed? It's time for lunch.

It's only a dollar with my gas purchase. A penny saved is a penny earned. Dotty, I saved two dollars. Today is dollaroff day.

You wasted my morning, Fred.

Ten minutes! It was only ten minutes, Dotty.

"Fred, do you mind if I go through the carwash?"

"Why should I mind?"

"It's hard to find a gas station that will pump gas these days. The Citgo on Eighteenth Avenue will, but they don't have a carwash. With all this rain it reminds me of the dust storms in the '30s. Look how dirty my car is."

"That dirt, Herman, is good Iowa topsoil, brought here by the rain storms. We are losing our topsoil and overloading our groundwater table. There will be some awful floods this summer."

"Here?"

"Mostly downstream in the flatlands."

"You know from everything, Fred."

"I know from experience. Remember the flood of 'sixty five? This one will be worse."

"Fred, I am sorry about Emily. First Dotty, and now Emily . . ."

"What can I do?"

"Keep busy, Fred. Busy is good."

"I write when I have free time."

"I liked your last story. The part about the old man having to retire. Now that was sad. I take it you don't put much faith in the golden years."

"You are right, Herman."

"A father shouldn't have to bury a child. That's too much. I can't even imagine . . .

"Thanks, Herman. I'll see you Monday morning."

"You're not coming tomorrow to say Kaddish?"

"I'll see. I need some time for myself. Maybe you are right, Herman. Maybe it would be better to follow the tradition, to go to shul, to pray, to recite the Kaddish with the Minyan."

"When you have troubles, being around people helps. That much I know."

"You are right, Herman."

"So who was at services?"

"Same old folks, Helen. Esther is back from Florida."

"Did you eat?"

"Only a bite of herring and Challah."

"What flavor yogurt do you want?"

"It doesn't matter. You choose."

"I'll split a blueberry with you. I set the table. I thought you would be hungry."

"I spoke to George. Our girls won the twelve and under school tennis championship."

"That's nice."

Emily played number two on the highschool tennis team. She and

If I Could Sleep . . .

Naomi Karp won the girls' doubles in the Rockville open. Emily's trophies clustered around the TV in the upstairs den. Dotty noodged Emily to take them with her, but she never did.

Whenever Emily came home for a visit, she would pull down the Murphy bed and sleep in the den. Don't ask me why she preferred the den when there are two empty bedrooms across the balcony.

Emily was an insommiac who visited sleep with the blackandwhite movies on all night television.

"Emily's tennis trophies are still up there in the den."

"That is exactly what I mean, Fred. Throw something out. Begin with the trophies. Nobody wants them. Your house looks like the address is on Memory Lane."

"That nineteenfifties furniture is very valuable. The chrome frame aqua vinyl couch in the den is an original Herman Miller."

"Okay, keep your couch. Throw out something! Who will miss Emily's tennis trophies? They're just dust catchers."

"Did I tell you Esther is back?"

"She still inviting you to dinner?"

"I don't go."

Esther is like those brown pelicans that sit in the mangroves waiting to dive, to swallow the little fish.

"Why don't you go?"

"I value my life."

"What's that?"

"I said I value my freedom.

"I had a shot of whiskey at the Kiddush."

"That's good, Fred. You know, you could drink a bit more. Maybe that would help with your pain. George has a cocktail before dinner.

"Your mail is on the desk."

"Any good news?"

"I didn't open it. I only sorted it."

"You could open it, I don't care."

"I don't open your mail!"

"Helen, I know you don't. Never mind about the mail. I'll open it tonight."

"Why don't you wash up. Lunch will be ready in a few minutes."

"I want to go through the Alumni News."

"Time to eat, Fred. Any news from the outside world?"

"I lost another classmate. But Jesse was an old man of seventy four."

I, on the other hand . . .

"You always read the obituaries first?"

"Usually."

"My dear brother, you have become a creature of strange habits. Shall I put your fingerbowl on the table?"

Fred, did you have to wash your hands in your waterglass?

I wasn't washing my hands, Dotty, all I did was dip my napkin in the waterglass.

You washed your hands with the best napkin. That is disgusting! Washing hands at the table!

Rinsing the fingers after the meal, before we say Grace. Our ancient and noble custom. Nobody thought it was disgusting when we ate at that fancy Chinese restaurant.

Dinner in the diner, nothing could be finer. Fiveoclock Rocket from Chicago to Rockville. Dinner at six with fingerbowls, red carnations in silver vases, your written dinnerorder picked up by a black waiter in whitestarched livery. Thank you Mr. Stern. So nice to see you again Mrs. Stern.

Give my regards to Mrs. Thornton.

If I Could Sleep . . .

That was a very generous tip that you gave Jim Thornton. We travel coach to save eight dollars, and you overtip Jim Thornton.

It's not easy being away from home.

Jim is home every night. You know that, Fred. He gets off in Rockville same as we do.

"Blessed are You, Lord, our God, King of the universe, who brings forth bread from the earth."

"This afternoon, you could go out to the Y, take your swim."

It's still Shiva, Helen, and anyway, I don't swim on the Sabbath.

"It's family swim this afternoon. Too many little kids in the lanes."

"Since when do you mind kids?"

"When the girls were little we used to go to the Y every Saturday afternoon. Say, did I tell you the taxes went down on the six acres in Junction?"

"Is that Good news?"

"Dotty was right."

"About what?"

"That I would never build in Junction."

You are a completely stupid naive man Fred. Stupid because you don't learn, because you won't learn. You are an undesirable in Junction. Persona non grata! You are the big city slicker who bought a corner of their little world. You took a cornfield and wanted to build rental housing. You have no constituency in Junction. Nobody loves you. The mayor hates you, the city attorney despises you for your persistence. The city manager wishes you would go somewhere else.

I promise, Dotty, I'll give up, sell the six acres.

You are an untrustworthy individual, Fred. You promised me!

I didn't ask for the meeting.

No, your real estate agent did!

I didn't, Dotty!

Alex B. Stone

I can't communicate with you, Fred. I yell, I scream, you don't hear me. Go to the meeting with the city engineer. You'll be insulted again. You don't even know when you are being insulted. That is why I want you to go get rid of the six acres. Give it away!

The new sewerline should go right by the property. As soon as the sewer is put in we can sell out.

You were right, Dotty.

"You know, Helen, sometimes I think Dotty should have run the business. She would have, too, if she hadn't hated it . . . "

Go take your Sabbath nap. I'll give you a heating pad for your leg. I heard you walking around all night."

"I'm okay, Helen. Thank you."

Had to put on my TENS unit last night. Bellypack with the red eyes that twinkle when the 7.2 volt battery is turned on. One electrode on my back, one on my thigh just above the knee. The two leads, one from each leg, plug into the powerpack.

Dr. Hellman, sixhundred dollars for a TENS unit . . . !

I'll write a prescription for it. Fred, you must get some sleep.

Dr. Hellman, the TENS unit can be duplicated for 20 dollars.

Medicare will pay. Turn the TENS unit on when your legmuscles ache and spasm. That little bit of a shock wave will stop the pain.

The batterypack looks like something out of a 1940s comicbook. Spacecadet Fred Stern zooming in for duty, Captain. Captain Buck Rogers and his rocketbelt five days a week in the Rockville Argus. Flying through the air with greatest of ease. Space with greatest of grace. Daring young cadet.

"Go lie down, Fred. You look tired."

Need to go swimming in the little pool 88 degrees Fahrenheit. Reserved mornings for senior citizens. Aquacize class. Enrollment limited to arthritics and poststroke patients. At noon my twentytwo minutes of laptime. Breaststroke up, backstroke back, crawl up, backstroke back. Up and back. The sun lights the pooltiles, reflects into the eddies and swirls made when my arms and hands pull me slowly down and forward. Kick off the side with my left leg—the good leg, the better leg, up and back. I swim off course because of my weak right leg, invade the second lane in which Ed Haines is exercising his postcoronarybypass heart. I stop, stand up in the three feet of water, take off my blue Leader swimgoggles.

Sorry, Ed. I was thinking of something else.

Ed, his ears plugged with swimwax, hasn't heard me. I will apologize to him in the shower or when we are dressing.

"You up already?"
"I got cold."
"I put the extra blankets in the closet."
"I know."
"You want some tea? It will warm you up."
"No thank you, Helen."
"Try to go back to sleep."
"I want to write some letters."

Where shall I go?
Where are you from?
Where from?
From Rockville,
Rockville on the Mississippi.
There are Jews there?
Fewer each year.
How did you end up in Rockville?'
That is another story.
Tell me . . .

Alex B. Stone

You are a totally unreliable, untrustworthy, individual....
I loved you, Dotty . . . Kiss me, Dotty.
I am not washed, Fred . . .

Chapter Nineteen

"What are you so busy with?"

"Writing in my journal."

"You keep a diary?"

"It's more like a weekly recording of events. Not personal like a diary—a record of business in progress or what happened to me."

It has been eight days since Emily's funeral. Helen has been very supportive. Edith and Edna went home Tuesday afternoon. My fibromyalgia in exacerbation, which I attribute to grief. Sleeping about the same. Poorly or not at all.

Still raining. Downtown, roof leaking into fifthfloor hallway. Have delayed new roof for twelve years. I hope it will go another winter. Only leaks when it rains. Air conditioning only fritzes in the summer. The steam boiler only blows in the winter.

"Helen, I think a cup of tea is a good idea."

"That's what I said, Fred."

"There is all sorts of cake. What kind do you want, carrot cake, sponge cake or rhubarb pie."

"Did you keep a record of who brought what? I want to write to thank them."

"Make up your mind, Fred."

"I'll have some of your strawberry jam and Challah."

If I Could Sleep . . .

"You going to the Mincha, to the service?"

"I don't think so."

"I'll hold supper if you want to go, say Kaddish."

"I do enough praying.

"Rains all afternoon. Just before sunset the sun comes out!"

"Every storm has a silver lining."

"Thank you, Helen. I'm glad you told me."

"You don't have to get huffy with me."

"Clichés drive me crazy."

"Optimism is genetically imprinted. Something we inherit."

"That's how I must have gotten mine, Helen. I surely didn't get it from experience."

"You were optimistic when you went into business."

"It was a very long time ago, two lifetimes ago."

"You did well."

"Dotty didn't think so."

"Dotty had everything she could wish for."

"Not everything. Dotty wanted the profitability of business without the risk taking. She longed for the peace of mind of being married to a grade fifteen civil servant.

"She never said that to me."

"She told me every time I discussed business with her."

"Thank God George and I don't talk about business."

"George is smarter than I am. I thought Dotty should know, should be involved in the business just in case. You know, Helen, the husbands are supposed to die first."

"You know from everything, Fred."

"Look at our congregation. Look at our demographics. We have widows from sixty to ninety. Some of our widows have been married two, three times."

"Your voice is crackling."

"It's the fluid from my lungs coming up into my throat."

Clear your throat, Fred. It is very annoying for those listening to you on the telephone.

Yes, Dotty, I will, Dotty.

Don't clear your throat into the telephone, Fred. If you are going to make those gargling sounds, cover the mouthpiece.

Yes, Dotty.

"Yes, Dotty."

"I am Helen, your sister. Dotty was your wife."

"I know that."

"Fred, there are days when I think . . ."

"I know, that I am totally out of it."

"You are not listening, Fred. Fred, you don't listen to what anyone else says. You don't let me finish."

"Okay, finish, say it!"

"Forget it. You won't hear me. Your mind is a thousand miles away. Are you writing a story in your head? . . . Fred?"

"What?"

"You look so distracted."

"I was thinking about Emily. After I am gone there will be no one to say Kaddish for her."

"You still have Edith and Edna and their children to be . . ."

"By now all my daughters should have had children. Emily should have had a son to say Kaddish for her, not her father."

"Thank God Emily still has a father."

"You are right, Helen."

"You want to talk about Emily, talk. You will feel better for doing it."

"I would like to cry! Just sit down and cry."

Emily is now a brass memorial plate on the farthest wall to the left of the sanctuary. Hebrew name. Chaia bat Dvorah. Hebrew date of death 4 Iyar. For a onehundreddollar donation her name will be read, memorialized, after the Torah reading on the Monday or Thursday closest to her date of death. It will be read as long as there is a Bnai Jacob Congregation in Rockville and ten people to gather for the morning prayer service.

"I tried to cry, Helen, I tried, I couldn't. When Dotty died I cried. Not much but I cried."

For Emily I moan in pain. I hurt with all my heart, with all my soul. Emily, formed from my body, from Dotty's too, yes, from Dotty's and our grandparents and our forefathers. Emily was our first miracle.

She is so small, Dotty.

I bathed the girls. Once or twice I even diapered them. Dotty said so. I remember Dotty saying so. I don't remember bathing Emily or Edith or Edna. I remember the cars we bought for them when they went off to college. Maybe if I try to remember it will come back when they were little, when they needed me.

"You cried at the funeral, Fred. You did, I was there, believe me."

"Everything is going too fast; it's Saturday night almost. Time to go to bed. Helen, I am going to take a bath."

"The whirlpool help?"

"Who knows."

"What's the matter?"

"It's my left hand, no circulation and hardly any feeling."

"Do something about it, Fred."

Going to soak my hand in a whirlpool of soothing, healing, warm Mississippi River water...

"Fred?"

"Yes, Helen."

"There is a brass pin on Emily's dress—that one that she had in Austria. I saw it when I hung up her dress."

"I know."

"The pin is so simple, so beautiful. I know the insert is only green glass, but it's an absolutely perfect specimen of turn of the century

American jewelry design."

"So?"

"It would compliment the one you gave me for my sixtieth birthday."

"The pins are not worn in sets."

"I know. I would wear this pin on my dresses like Emily did and leave the other on my British tweed walking suit."

"Say it. You would like to have Emily's antique pin."

"As a memory of Emily."

"I gave it to her."

"All the better to remember you and Emily."

"Take it. I still have all of Dotty's brass and glass pins."

"How many do you have?"

"More than a dozen."

"Dotty wore them all?"

"Most of them."

You, know, Helen, when I started collecting those trinkets they could be bought for two dollars at the Galesburg Antique Fair—vintage American jewelry, brass on brass, finest quality. I bought those pins when no one knew what they were. When no one wanted grandma's fiveanddime pins and buckles and bracelets. I have two bracelets you have never seen, Helen. Look at the filigree work, look at the clasps, Helen. I also have a locket with a place for two pictures. That I am saving for our first granddaughter. Dotty's and my first granddaughter.

Placed a snapshot of Emily in another one—a brass memorial locket, a rarity. There are museums that would love to have my antique jewelry collection.

Give it to a museum.

"What are you going to do with Dotty's pins?"

"Give them to a museum."

"I would bet Edith and Edna would love to have them."

If I Could Sleep . . .

"I asked them."

"What did they say?"

"They said they didn't want them."

"Give them to me. That would be better than giving them to a museum!"

A collection of antique American jewelry, donated in the memory of Dorothy Stern of Rockville, Illinois. Twelve pins valued at threehundred dollars each. Equals thirtysixhundred dollars. Your receipt, Mr. Stern. Thank you, Mr. Stern. Don't forget to list your gift on your tax return.

"You are right, Helen. Better to keep things in the family."

For now I will wait. Edith will change her mind. Edna will leaf through her Exmasedition of the Neiman Marcus catalog. Diverse and fashionable antique brass pins, never two alike. My dad has dozens of these. Dad, how were you so perceptive? You bought furniture designed by McCobb and Eames, modernist painting and antique jewelry, Inuit sculpture and German expressionist prints and limited edition art catalogs . . . Tell me, Dad, how did you know what to buy?

One day I'll tell you. We'll go for a walk, you and Edith and I, on the Sanibel beach. We will walk east to the lighthouse.

My daughters beside me, the surfsounds, the gulls swoop and whirl and return to the beach. The pelican with the long yellow beak diving into the surf. It's a clear morning, the sun glints off the gulf.

It was in the early 'Fifties when I came back from Korea. When your mother and I were married I was still in the airforce. We were living in a furnished basement apartment. We hung a maroon made in Belgium oriental carpet to cover the cracks and damp of the concrete wall, painted the bare concrete floor barnred, nailed butcher paper onto the exposed ceiling studs.

Papa, when did you get the Kasvan rug?

I sold a Worthington Whittridge painting to buy that rug. Your mother wanted a beigeandblue oriental for our living room.

Alex B. Stone

Papa, who is Worthington Whittridge?

Study my child, study American art history and you shall learn of Whittridge and Gifford, of Moran and Bierstadt.

What did you study, Papa?

Me? I studied economics.

How did you learn so much about art?

Home study. Reading art catalogs and going to museums.

Papa, we did not enjoy being dragged through museums.

I didn't know that, my daughters. I apologize, my daughters. I thought it was good for you. Enrichment. I gave you what I thought you needed. A common error, no doubt, of poor parents.

Were you poor, Papa?

Not by the time you girls were born. Up From Poverty: the Life of Fred B. Stern, bomberpilot, economist, builder, philanthropist, now long retired. A man who once thought he would never live to write.

"Fred, turn up the heat before you take your bath."

"It's going to be clear tomorrow."

"How do you know?"

"I saw the sky, sunny and dry."

"Fred, don't lock yourself in."

In case you can't get up out of the tub, Helen will help you up. Fred you shouldn't be living alone. Fred, you need a keeper. I'll take a shower, and if I want to take a bath I'll take my portable phone so in case of an accident I can call nineoneone.

"After your bath, Fred, would you like a little hot milk? Hot milk and dry toast, you'll sleep better."

Fred! Why are you using your fingers to take out the toast? Use a fork. I told you a thousand time to use a fork. You will burn your hand. Fred, why are you using your left hand?

Left hand, right hand, what difference does it make, Dotty?

Fred, you planted the chrysanthemums where I can't see them.

I'll replant them tomorrow.

If I Could Sleep . . .

The chrysanthemums are still living, Dotty is gone.
"Who told you that milk helps sleep?"
"Everyone knows that."
Twelve minutes of whirlpool bath with jets at full force, soak your back and your hands, then your back exercises: twenty modified situps, ten leglifts, ten legsapart and ten backbends, touch the floor, ten kneebends. Stretch! Stretch! Trunk to the left, trunk to the right and back. A halfmilligram valium before bedtime. Does it help? I don't know. So why do you do your exercises? Why do you take your pills? Why? I am afraid to stop, afraid of more pain, afraid to die. You are looking good, Fred.
Considering the circumstances, I look terrific.

"Fred, you okay in there?"
"Fine, Helen, just fine."
"You coming out?"
"I'll be right out."
"I'll make the milk."
"Please, Helen. No hot milk."
"Can you get up?"
"I had a grab bar put in."
"When?"
"When I decided on hip surgery."

Hear O Israel, the Lord is our God, the Lord is One. Blessed be our God from Whom all goodness comes. Protect me and guide me. I thank You for my life that is in Your care.

God, Emily was only fortytwo.

Our Father and King, be gracious unto us. Answer us, deal kindly with us and love us.

May the Lord bless you and guard you. May He Who establishes peace in His heavens grant peace unto us and unto all Israel and say ye Amen.

Chapter Twenty

On the bureau the greeneyed clock says 1:06. In the kitchen the white face of the microwave reads 1:08. At the sink in front of the kitchen window in one swallow I down four ounces of chilled Chardonnay. At the end of the drive the mist glows orange in the streetlight.

Left hand under head back to sleep. Twothirty two Tylenol and a halfglass of water, then the 4:30 walk to the bathroom. At 5:40 the chase. A sweating bicyclist pumping pumping up and down a hill in vain pursuit of a steamengine.

Awake with a headache, a backache, a numbtingling left hand, throw off my two cotton blankets, make for the shower. The hot water rinses the sweat from my head. I turn my back to the spray, begin my stretches, eventually reach the floor with the fingers of both hands, shut off the shower, wrap myself in my terry robe, apply shavingcream to my grey face.

Helen at the door.

"You woke me. You turn on the water downstairs, it sounds twice as loud upstairs. You know that."

"I forgot. I guess I have just been alone too long."

"You are a totally inconsiderate man. Where are you rushing to? Why don't you do like a normal human being, read your Sunday

Times, make yourself a cup of tea and not wake me up? It's Sunday!"

"You are right, Helen."

"So I am right, but you don't think of anyone else, you just do your own thing."

"I didn't mean to wake you."

"You did whether you meant to or not."

"You didn't sleep well, Helen?"

"You walk around all night. You slammed the refrigerator door."

"I am sorry. You are such a light sleeper . . ."

"I'm not a light sleeper. You are a very noisy man. Every night you are up, you are down. I am not complaining, I am only saying."

"I did not say you complained."

"Would you like some breakfast, Helen? I'll quarter an orange for you."

"You expect me to do as you do? Stand over the sink, spit the pits into the disposal?"

"You don't have to do what I do. Do you want an orange?"

"I'll have some juice."

"Grape Nuts or bagel?"

"What are you having, Fred?"

"Whatever you like."

"Cereal is fine."

"Okay, shake out what you want."

"What's the weather report?"

"More rain."

"Rain, rain, go away! Little Helen wants to play. You want to go to services?"

"Me and the old men?"

"We get widows, too."

"No, not for me. You want coffee, Fred?

"If you are making some for yourself."

"What's in the Times?"

"Same old bad news. But there is a section on women's fashion in the 'Forties."

"May I have that?"

"All yours, Helen."

"Claire McCardell, the trendsetting sportswear designer of the '40s. Her natural look in sportswear freed the postwar woman. What happened to Dotty's Claire McCardell dresses? Dotty had a dress like that."

"She did?"

"Those Claire McCardells are now worth a fortune. A couple of years ago the Metropolitan Museum had an entire exhibition devoted to the nineteenforties designers."

"The dresses are upstairs all hanging in a row, tagged and identified by Dotty."

"Thank God she didn't throw them out when she couldn't wear them."

"Dotty didn't like getting fat. Dotty knew the value of what she had."

"What are you going to do with the dresses? How many are there?"

"I don't know."

"How much are they worth?"

"I don't know."

"What are you going to do with them?"

"I told the girls they were there.'

"That's not doing anything."

"It's a step."

"You going to services?"

"It is not until nine o'clock on Sunday."

"Did you read the card that came from Rockville College?"

"I'll read it when I write my thankyous."

"Someone named Jay Cook took a lot of trouble. You got a long personal note."

"Development officers watch the obituaries. In a couple of weeks Cook will want to take me out to lunch, see if Emily left the college anything."

"Emily didn't go to Rockville."

"She sent them something every year for our lecture fund."

"You endowed that."

"A few of our friends add to it."

"Do you know how much is in there?"

"No."

"So why do you add to it?"

"Sometimes we use the money to help the kids who want to go to Israel to work on a dig. They don't ask for much, usually not more than a couple of thousand dollars."

"That's a lot of money."

"Not as much as it used to be, Helen."

"You buying any paintings since the prices have fallen?"

"I should, but I haven't. It's the damn insurance rates. Insurance rates go up and up. I never had a loss, and each year our insurance goes up ten percent."

"If values go down how could rates go up?"

"Minimum premiums, Helen. Lloyd's took a beating, so now I have minimum premiums on lower market values. The whole thing is stupid. That keeps insured values higher than the replacement value. Say we had a loss: Lloyd's would pay more than replacement value.

Stupid! Lloyd's should know their business."

"I don't understand it."

"Well, don't ask me. I'll take a key, Helen. I am walking over. Back in an hour."

2

"What's new at services?"

"The Rabbi put his hands on my head, said the few prescribed words to raise me from my Shiva."

"So now we could go for a drive?"

"You want to go out to the tree farm? I'd like to see the new growth."

"It's wet out there."

"I'll give you some boots."

"Whose? Dotty took a size ten. I take an eight."

"I'll stuff the boots with paper. You won't lose them. The logging roads are no longer muddy, not since the prairie grass has taken over."

"Sure. You on your cane, me swimming in Dotty's boots. We make a great pair."

"I'll buy you a pair of size eights."

"We'll see. Maybe the sun will come out."

"I doubt it. Not today."

"What do you usually do on Sunday?"

"Work in the yard, then write. Sometimes I go to a movie."

"We could go to a movie."

"Not for another month. Not until Sheloshim."

"You are becoming a religious fanatic."

"It's our tradition."

"Tradition, tradition. Nothing changes in Rockville."

"Each year we have more widows. We have as many widows as we have families. One hundred and forty widows, one hundred and forty families."

"How many single men?"

"About twenty."

"All like you? All afraid of women?"

Women who kill men with love. I would love for you to clean out the gutters. I would love for you to peel off the wall paper. Old joke.

"I don't know anything about anybody else's business."

"Don't you have a singles scene?"

Downtown Rockville on Friday night. Men and women lying to each other about their jobs, their income, their children, their hopes, their ambitions, drinking and forgetting until Monday.

"I'm too old."

"You could take a widow out for a drink."

"I don't know any widows."

"One hundred and forty widows, you don't know one!"

"I don't know a widow I would want to have dinner with."

"They all too stupid?"

"I didn't say that."

"So what is it?"

"They will all end up wanting the same thing."

"What?"

"A more perfect Fred Stern in a more perfect world."

"You don't give yourself a chance, and what is worse, you don't give anyone else a chance."

"I've had my chance. So have most people of a certain age. Things are what they are."

Fred Stern as is. A man as good as he can be, a kind and generous man. Willing enough to please but somehow never quite succeeded. As Dotty said when I burned the toast. Everything you touch turns to dreck.

"Things are what they are."

"That is arrogant, Fred. With that attitude we would all still be living in caves."

"What do you want me to do, Helen, start over fresh?"

Face it, Fred. You are a lousy manager and you really don't write very well either. You are into your own bellybutton, into yourself. Self, self, self. Dotty was right. I didn't run my construction company any better than I do my office building. All I do is complain. Why didn't you join the Downtown Development Corporation? They would be delighted to entertain your ideas on how much parking the downtown needs.

I don't like meetings.

Meetings take time from yourself, from contemplating your navel.

I've paid my dues. I no longer have to do what I don't enjoy. Always the easy way. The members of your luncheon club standing in the cold, ringing bells in front of the Venture Store. Please give to the Salvation Army Christmas fund. Feed the poor of Rockville. Toys for the abandoned children of Rockville. A small gift for the unwed mothers of Rockville. You, Fred, send a check. It's my arthritic hands. It's my back. My hip. My feet freeze. Excuses. You sit home and write stories no one reads.

We all have different priorities. I am a very generous person.

Sure, you write checks. You don't give of yourself.

"Besides: who would want a piece of me, Helen? Whom am I depriving?"

"A caring woman. A woman who is not afraid to give of herself. Your trouble, Fred, is you were married to an unhappy woman."

Fred, I know we can be happy together. We will be happy. Believe me. Let's try. What do we have to lose? Only our aloneness . . .

Fred, you don't play bridge? How unusual.

I play golf. No, I don't do games, no Scrabble, no Trivial Pursuit.

I could teach you.

I don't really care to learn. I don't play cards. No, how shall I put it? I don't have time for cards.

What are you so busy with?

Making plans. Planning for the future. I am negotiating on several longterm leases for office rental space.

I understand the rental market is depressed.

I have several very innovative ideas; leasebacks, condominium sales, rehab for tax credits...

That should keep you very busy.

It does. I suppose I could let my property manager take over. Then you and I could travel, visit my publisher in California . . .

You have a publisher? On the West Coast?

Actually, no. My novel is under consideration. The publisher has assigned it to an editor. If the editor . . .

"Fred, lunch!"

"Coming, Helen. I just want to wash my hands.

"If you like, Helen, we could drive up to Junction. I would like to see what the low places in the cornfield look like."

"Can't we just go for a drive to nowhere? Just along the river and back."

"On the way back from Junction we could stop at the Cove for homemade pie and coffee."

"That's you, Fred, a simple Sunday afternoon drive becomes an expedition with destinations and rest stops."

"What is the harm, Helen?"

"I give up, Fred. Can't you just keep things simple?"

"I'll do what you like, but I don't understand what's wrong with eating pie at the Cove. We can drive through Loud Thunder Forest Preserve."

Right on 31st Avenue, over the railroadtracks. On the left the vacant warehouse and offices of Cummins Diesel. On the right, the municipal landfill. Straight ahead to the left of the marina the Rock River empties into the Mississippi. There is the river—see it as we go over the bridge. The Mississippi has risen. A few more feet and all barge traffic will have to stop when the rollerdams are opened to permit the snowmelt from Minnesota and Wisconsin to flow through. West on the Andalusia road, up the wooded hills into the Loud Thunder Forest Preserve.

"Shall I stop at Lake George?"

"Why?"

"You are right, Helen. There is no need to stop."

"I only asked what is there to see at Lake George?"

"It could be that the excavation for the new storage shed has begun."

"My, how exciting . . . !"

After the war, when I first started driving these roads, no highway beyond Andalusia. No State Bank, no Lake George, no skilift.

"We could climb the observation tower. There is a fine view of the Andalusia Islands."

"No thanks, Fred. I am satisfied right here in the car. At my age I don't climb anything."

"A few days of sunshine would be a Godsend. This bottom land doesn't drain well. See the water standing? We are about half way to Junction. I could turn around or cross the Mississippi at Muscatine and then it's only a few miles to Junction."

"What's in Muscatine?"

If I Could Sleep . . .

"The Helen Musser Art Museum."

"What is on exhibit?"

"I don't know."

"Let's turn around, I know you want to go to services."

"I have enough time to run up to Junction. It won't take any longer if I come back on the Interstate."

"Do as you like, Fred. You will anyway."

"There is no harm to it."

"No, just keep on doing your own thing."

"Here we are, Helen. That didn't take long to get to Junction."

"You own all this land?"

"It's only six acres."

"Is it valuable?"

"The taxes are ninety two dollars a year. It costs me more to fill out the tax return than I get for my share of the crop.

"Why don't you sell, get rid of it?"

"The sewer is coming."

"When?"

"In two, three, four years."

"How long have you been waiting?"

"Twelve, thirteen years."

Fred, you are a lousy manager.

Dotty, no one gets a hundredpercent of anything.

So the deal in Junction to build apartments went sour. So you threw good money after bad. You wasted legal fees, design fees, engineering fees. You never know when to quit.

It's my character defect, Dotty. I can't help it.

You don't use your head, Fred. You don't know when you can't succeed. Isn't any bigcity Jewboy like you going to get any cooperation from the city fathers of a onehorse town like Junction.

My rental development would have provided affordable, equal opportunity housing to a town that needs it.

Junction doesn't want Fred Stern, can't you understand that? Need has nothing to do with it, Fred.

Junction would benefit from the increase in tax base.

Fred, you don't understand. You are a bigcity Jew.

Dotty. Rockville is not a big city.

"Which way home, Helen? Back along the river or on the interstate?"

"Along the river."

"Helen, do you remember when we went on picnics to Loud Thunder?" Mama had a favorite parkbench. In the meadow beside the abandoned log cabin. After lunch we walked along the shore. Once we saw a white pelican. "Do you remember? Do you know, I haven't been on a picnic in thirty years!"

Not since Emily bought the picnic table for me with the first money she earned. The picnic table that is in the backyard, the redwood one that rests on the twobyfours just to the left of the burn pile. Not the folding one that is tipped over on the fence. Dotty bought that foldable bench for extra seating at our 4th of July backyard picnics.

"Fred, do you ever eat in your gazebo? Dotty used to serve such beautiful teas out there."

"No, not since Dotty died. What's the sense of one man preparing a tray for himself."

"Fred, will you stop by HyVee? I want to get some onions for the grilled hamburgers. Hamburgers okay for tonight?"

"Whatever you like, Helen."

"When was the last time you used your gas grill?"

"Is it dirty?"

"No, it looks as if it has never been used."

"Emily bought it for me for my birthday. She had it assembled and delivered as a surprise, all set up and ready to go. There is an extra tank of propane in the garage if you need it."

"Why would I run out of propane if you haven't used the grill?"

"I guess you wouldn't."

"You need beer, Fred. You get the beer, I'll get the onions."

HyVee, a full service supermarket managed by an Afroamerican. 25 centsacup self service coffee to be drunk in booths under a glassroofed alcove overlooking the handicapped parking. Coffee with nominally homemade takeout deliproducts. Friedchicken, roastbeef, lunchmeats, pickledherring, coleslaw, pickledbeets. A place to meet and eat for the older singles of Rockville.

Not the elderly. The elderly are served by Meals on Wheels, delivered to your home by caring volunteers.

The restaurant of choice for aftermorningprayer breakfasts. Two eggs over, toast and coffee, a buck ninetynine.

"Fred! Why don't you join us for breakfast."

"Thank you, Rabbi. I have already eaten."

I know. How can I eat before services. How can I fill my stomach before praising God for the goodness of his gifts, for my life, for my food, for my waking, for making me a Jew. It's like I tell you, Rabbi, I have learned to aspire to less than complete asceticism. If it bothers God that I still have a little appetite after waking up from a sleepless night, I will accept my demerits without an argument.

"Why are you always in such a hurry, Fred? Come sit down with us."

"I'd love to, Rabbi, but I can't. I'm on a mission and my sister is keeping an eye on me from the vegetable department."

"It was good seeing you at Minyan this morning, Fred. We barely made it without you."

"I know. If one of us can't make it it's not like you don't notice."

"Fred! You didn't get the beer?"

"There was no dark beer."

"You know I like a beer with my hamburgers!"

"Sorry, Helen. I'll be right back. I know, Miller Lite. Sorry, I forgot."

Dollar cheaper at Walgreen's.

You are right, Dotty. I'll pick up the beer on the way home.

Fred, buy a couple of sixpacks and, Fred, buy some lager for me. Fred, we need stamps. Fred, buy a whole roll.

I am at the postoffice two, three times a week. Why should I invest 29 dollars with the postoffice?

Fred, send the gifts to the girls in France by air.

Dotty, that will cost six dollars.

What's the matter, Fred, you can't afford it? Did you insure the birthday presents?

I sent the gifts by air.

So you saved another two dollars by not buying the insurance. You are getting worse, Fred, worse.

It's not economical to spend eight dollars to insure two L.L. Bean nightgowns worth 20 dollars.

Fred, what if the package gets lost?

The French postoffice is very efficient.

You know from everything, don't you, Fred?

Had to be frugal once, now it's etched into me.

"Fred, we could pick up from the deli. The broiled turkey legs look very nice. You ever tried the fried chicken? You like fried chicken."

If I Could Sleep . . .

I have joined the HyVee Dining Club. After a leisurely repast of pickledherring, coleslaw and slicedcoldturkey topped off by breadpudding, I visit the service counter where I rent my 99¢ overnight videotape for that evening's viewing.

Mr. Stern, are you pleased to have joined the HyVee Diner's Community? Yes indeed I am. Very pleased. Very pleased indeed.

"Did you hear me, Fred? Why not pick up something from the deli counter?"

"Whatever you say, Helen."

"Sure, Fred. Really, you are hopeless!"

Hopeless and helpless, Helen! Don't know what I will do when my seamstress retires. Who will turn my collars, put in new pockets in my slacks, let out my jackets, sew up my cuffhems?

Elinore will not be retiring until next October. Henry has somebody. I'll have to ask Henry who does his repairs. Henry dresses every bit as well as I do.

"Did I tell you, Helen, I tried to buy a new suit last time I was in Chicago? I found one exactly what I was looking for to replace the suit I bought in nineteen sixty five."

"So what happened, they wouldn't sell it to you?"

"You know that today the same suit costs four times what it did in nineteen sixty five?"

"Fred, do you have four times the earnings you had in nineteen sixty five?"

"Most I ever spent, and it didn't fit."

"So, where is the suit?"

"Wait. I went for two fittings. With each alteration I looked worse. The shoulder padding was bunched up, the jacket didn't fall right and the trousers crept to the right. Beautiful fabric—not as good as what I bought in nineteen sixty five, but a beautifully finished imported woollen worsted."

"So, where is your suit?"

"The suit I sent back. Wore it once, and I sent it back. I got a hundred percent credit. For thirty five years I buy my clothes in the same store. This is the first I didn't look good, and for that kind of money I should look good."

"You have to buy yourself a suit, Fred."

Are you going to buy a suit or aren't you?

I'll wear my blazers. I have three blazers. That's enough.

You do look elegant in your blazers . . . .

Thank you, Dotty.

"Fred, you need a suit that fits you. That suit you wore at the funeral looked like you bought it in a second hand store."

"It's a fine suit, Helen. I wore my dark grey herringbone wool to Emily's funeral. It's only ten years old."

"The lapels are too narrow, the trousers are a little tight at the waist and too narrow at the ankles."

"Who looks at an old man?"

"That's enough of that old age nonsense! Save that for Edith and Edna. They told me how all you talk to them about is yourself. Why the self pity, Fred? That's what the girls said. Either Dad talks about himself or he talks business. That's boring to your daughters."

"What should I talk to them about?"

"A man of your education and knowledge! Talk to them about art, literature, the theatre, music, the movies."

Dear Edith, Dear Edna,

Next fall there will be a Max Ernst retrospective exhibition at the Chicago Art Institute. It's a rare opportunity to view European surrealism. Ernst was one of the founders of Dada. Why don't I drive into Chicago? I would love to have you join me for the viewing, just for a few hours. We could have lunch and if you had the time, perhaps you could help me pick out a suit. I haven't bought a suit since Mama died.

You are whining, Dad. Please don't whine.

If I Could Sleep . . .

Brooksbrothers is just across Michigan Avenue. I do value your opinion, Edna, or I wouldn't ask you to join me. If you have the time, we could look at the Shapiro collection of works on paper, only if you wish, of course.

Dad, it's always the same with you, another expedition. I don't have a half a day. I could manage a couple of hours, but with you, it's an expedition.

How about lunch at the Berghoff? A sandwich and a dark beer?

I don't want a Max Ernst catalog. I have had enough surrealism. You keep the catalog, Dad. I bought it for you.

I really don't know how to speak to my daughters.

You are a very interesting man. Be natural, don't try to entertain, don't try so hard to please them. Listen, Fred. Learn to listen, let the girls talk.

Yes, Dotty.

Dear Emily,

I would be delighted to be your guide to the American Collection of the Chicago Art Institute. You wrote of your interest in women painters. Do you know Doris Lee's work? In the '30s Doris Lee painted regional scenes of West Virginia, Western Illinois, exploring home and hearth. We will look at Thanksgiving at Grandma's, which she did in 1936. It is more a genre painting than a landscape, but still a fine painting. Thank God they haven't included any of her work from the '50s, when she was too much influenced by Milton Avery. Her colors flattened, her subjects, mostly still, geometric forms, floated and frowned in beds of grim greens and blues. Are you familiar with Milton Avery? His best period was in the Nineteensixties. He did a wonderful series of seaside watercolors. Fulllength, mature women in profile, silhouetted, suspended, in a sea of sunshine, sitting on the beach, standing on decks, overlooking the noonblue sea. Happy women, beyond the cares of childrearing, enjoying a chat, an afternoon of icedtea and sun and their grandchildren.

How do you know all this, Dad?

I visit galleries, go to exhibitions, read catalogs. Would you like a catalog of the American Collection?

Yes, thank you so much.

Not at all, you are welcome. De nada.

You speak Spanish, too?

"Did you notice how many old people and Blacks there were in the supermarket?"

"Marketing, it's all in the marketing, Helen."

HyVee identified its market and went after it. Now that Western Illinois is deindustrialized, aging is our leading industry. Phenomenal growth in the last twelve years. HyVee's employees are shareholders. That forestalls union tzuris. The girls at the servicecounter will put stamps on old ladies' letters, accept payment for their utilitybills and sell them a lotteryticket. Marketing is where it's at, Helen.

"You know, Helen, it's funny. If there was demand for office space in Rockville, I would have a full building. Then I could sell out, join you in New York—or better yet, real estate values are down in Manhattan too. I could buy a little one bedroom one bath condo pied a terre on Sutton Place. We could go to the Metropolitan Museum, the Frick, the Morgan . . ."

"You are so enthusiastic about living in New York, why haven't you visited me in ten years?"

"Eight."

"Okay, eight."

"You are right, Dotty."

"I am Helen. You want to start up the barbecue?"

"Whatever you like, Helen."

"Don't you have an opinion?"

"Not about when I eat."

"Fred, can you explain to me what it is with you becoming so religious? You remind me of those born agains."

"What else?"

"I don't know, something about you. Tolerant. Accepting. Secure. That I envy."

"I am not a born again."

"Yes, you are. Look at yourself, Fred. You lose a wife, you accept it. You lose a daughter; you accept that. You are planning a hip replacement—that's high risk surgery, it doesn't faze you for a minute. Your life is God given, isn't that it? And that protects you."

"Life is what it is."

"What is it?"

"It's my portion."

"Why are you so pleased with it?"

"I am not pleased with it but what can I do but pray?"

"What are you praying for?"

"It's a form of giving thanks."

"To whom?"

"To God."

"For what, Fred?"

"For what is!"

"I give up, Fred."

"The wind has shifted to the southwest. That should bring the humidity down. Maybe by tomorrow we can open the windows."

"I don't know how you can live in Rockville."

"It's home."

"You could live anywhere."

The fuchsia is blossoming. The yard is beginning to smell like a rainforest.

"I should cut the grass."

Alex B. Stone

"You should rest more."

"I haven't done anything for weeks."

For your spring lawn in Western Illinois, choose Ford's suretogrow, acclimated shadymix grassseed.

Your lawn is a miracle, Mr. Stern. I can't believe that you can grow any grass at all under those oaks.

Would you be kind enough to repeat that to Mrs. Stern? I'll call her.

Dotty, I was just visiting with the forester. You remember Steve Rush?

I just came by to look at the oaks, the six in your front yard. I have to agree with Mr. Stern. Topping the two on the west of the drive would add two, three sunlight hours onto your lawn.

I have been telling Fred to have the lawn aerated. Fred just doesn't listen to me.

Mrs. Stern, I don't believe aeration would help very much. Considering the shade your oaks spread, yours is as fine a lawn as possible. I don't know how your grass grows as well as it does.

Lots of reseeding, lots of work is what it takes. This spring I have spread 30 pounds of seed mixed into 600 pounds of topsoil.

Beautiful, just beautiful Kentucky blue grass.

I know why Steve Rush says such nice things about your lawn. It's because you collect acorns for him.

Native acorns are a very important part of oak reforestation. Before the settlers came . . .

Please, Fred, not another lecture.

"Isn't there a lawn service you could hire?"

"Why?"

"To make your life a little easier."

"The less you do the harder it gets."

When I start dating widows, that's when I'll hire my yard work done.

If I Could Sleep . . .

You'll hire your yardwork done long before then, Mr. Stern. After your hip replacement surgery no yardwork for six months, no twisting, no turning. For the first six weeks you will sleep on your back and then with a pillow between your legs. The pillow is to prevent your hip from dislocating and, Mr. Stern, no sex for eight weeks.

And after that, Doctor, is the sex optional or mandatory?

Dear Emily,

You asked about my favorite music. For piano music, Satie—always Satie—and Kurt Weil. For songs, Felicia Sanders sings Kurt Weil. Sanders died fifteen, twenty years ago. Edith Piaf is gone. Marlene Dietrich is dead. Patachou . . . Where is Patachou? Hildegard performs now and then. I have a complete set of Felicia Sanders on longplay records.

"Fred, you going to watch Masterpiece Theatre?"

"You go ahead. I'll get ready for bed."

Dear Dotty,

On our second honeymoon we can motor down to the Sanibel condo. Each morning is so different, each so tranquil, each so thankful. This morning the sun wore a copper cap of matching color like in the Comfort Inn sign. On our drive down, we'll listen to Satie or literary storytapes, or the story of your life.

Tell me your story, Fred. Then I'll tell you my story. It hasn't been easy for you, Fred, to lose a wife and then your daughter.

Tell me what do you dream about, Dotty? What is it you wish for?

Tell me, Fred, what shall we do with the rest of our lives?

Tell me, Dotty.

What do you wish? I am listening.

Alex B. Stone

Hold me, still my fear. I am afraid to die.

From death I know, Fred. Hold me. We will hold each other.

You will sleep in my arms. Put your head on my shoulder. You see, Fred, you went right back to sleep.

My North African amulet gold ring, Carnelian intaglio, with its outside border engraved with an acronym formed from the first letter of each word in the Hebrew blessing May the Lord Bless You and Keep You repeated in 19thcentury Arabic calligraphy in a central rosette, is set into gold with the ring's shanks carved into a floral design. I wear the Carnelian amulet ring only on the Sabbath and Holidays, keep it in my jewel box. A Carnelian stone set in a gold ring would make a man peaceful and slow to anger. Carnelian a defense against the evil eye. Carnelian cured depression, prevented pessimism. Dotty had a 19thcentury French Carnelian intaglio ring. On her ring the Greek gods rode in a chariot up up into the sky, ever higher, ever striving to reach the sun.

Don't bring any valuables to the hospital, Mr. Stern.

I will wear my class ring. Fred B. Stern, Ph.D., University of Chicago.

After the surgery, when you leave the hospital, you will need help, Mr. Stern. I will arrange for the visiting nurses to come in daily, do your wash up. But you really shouldn't be home alone, not for the first six weeks or so. I'll make the necessary arrangements.

I needed hip surgery to have a personal secretary?

"Fred? I thought you went to bed.

"Just thinking about tomorrow."

"There shouldn't be any surprises for you. You know what is in Emily's will."

"I have no idea of what is in Emily's will."

"Didn't Emily discuss her wishes with you when she asked you to be her executor?"

"No, not really."

"When are you going to the vault?"

"About ten."

"Do you want me to go with you?"

"If you like."

"I don't think you ought to be alone."

"You may be right, Helen."

Chapter Twenty-One

"It's only seven thirty, Fred; you have time for breakfast."

"I'll have breakfast when I come back from services. You don't have to wait . . ."

ঌ

"What took you so long?"

"We had the Monday reading from the Torah, then we had the special prayers for the new month. There were names to be read for this week's memorial list. The Talmud class was until nine fifteen. That is like always."

"You enjoy all that praying?"

"Some times I enjoy. Sometimes it's like any community obligation. Wearing."

"Anything you devote so much time to you should enjoy."

"You are right, Helen. King David says Serve God with joy."

"Why aren't you drinking your coffee?"

"It's too hot."

"I thought maybe you didn't like my coffee."

"It's better coffee than I ever made."

"Anytime you want to go downtown, I am ready, Fred."

"In a while, Helen. I'll call the office, see what is going on. Tell them I'll be a little late."

"You on a schedule?"

"I usually get in about nine thirty."

"Come along, Helen."

"I will say one thing for you, Fred. You do have a decent car."

"Two air bags, one for you, one for me, antilock brakes, adjustable leather seats and a moon roof. Who could ask for anything more?"

"I am surprised you spent the money."

"I bought safety. I didn't want my daughters to lose their father in a head on auto accident."

Right on 30th Street. Right onto 7th Avenue. Stop at the crosswalk where the Rockville College kids cross to get to their gym.

The redbuds are in bloom, the maples are leafing. Years ago, spring in Rockville smelled like lilacs. My gnarled lilac bush along the fence line is fifty years old if it is a day. Could be older. It still struggles to reach the sun. Still wants to live.

"You always drive this slowly, Fred?"

"It's the speed limit."

"Fred, would you say that yours and Dotty's was a happy marriage?"

Every time Helen and I are alone in a car. Are you happy? Are you sad? Are you mad?

"Why do you ask?"

"I read that men who had happy marriages usually remarry."

"It could be true. Dotty had some admirable qualities. She was a very caring mother, a wonderfully capable cook and housekeeper. Dotty had a very good head for organizing things. Everything in it's place, a place for everything. Woollen sweaters with woollen sweaters, cotton sweaters with cotton sweaters . . ."

Fred, isn't your life easier when your shirts are on one rack and your suits on another?

"So?"

"So what?"

"Why do you have to be different—so difficult?"

"Every time we are in a car, I get why, why."

"I want to understand so I can help."

"That is admirable."

"Don't get sarcastic on me, Fred."

"When Dotty died, after the mourning was over I wanted to prove I could manage on my own. Nothing very fancy. Just to get along."

"When Dotty died, I told George you would be married in a year, at the end of mourning. Then a year went by and another year. Now I don't understand. I don't understand you at all."

"What is to understand? Dotty was a hard act to follow. I let things drift, I drifted into my routines."

You can do better, Fred. I know you can.

Dotty, what is so important about doing better?

You don't try, Fred.

I try, Dotty. I just don't succeed.

"You are a successful man, Fred. You managed your life very well until Dotty died. Then you let ten years of your life go by."

"They went by very fast, Helen. It seems like a dream . . .

"Say it, Helen. It isn't natural for me to live alone. A healthy man your age has physical needs."

"Surely there were women who made overtures to you . . . ?"

There were. There are. Still feel the need for intimacy, but I get over that.

If I Could Sleep . . .

"Listen, Helen. I sleep with a TENS Unit. Two electrodes on my back, an electrode on each leg."

Fred, this time, don't attach your electrodes until after we make love.

"I will say one thing, Fred, we are communicating better than we used to. You are easier to talk to. I just don't think it's right you should be alone."

"Helen, did I or didn't I tell you that two anti hypertensive pills a day diminish libido?"

"Fred, really! All you to do is talk, talk, talk. More than anyone wants to hear—What's so funny? Why are you smiling?"

Fred, all you talk about is yourself. The conversation always has to come around to you.

Dotty, all I did was try to answer answer Joe's question.

So you spend an hour giving us the history of how, where, and why dissident religious groups set up utopian agrarian colonies in the midwest.

"Not much traffic in Rockville. Not like on the east coast. I could have learned to drive here."

"I offered to teach you, remember?"

"George wouldn't have let me use the car."

"As long as George is willing to drive you where you want to go…"

"I would have been more independent."

"Things were different fifty years ago."

"Some things I try not to remember. Especially about Mama and Papa."

"It's not easy for immigrants."

"Nor for immigrants' children."

"We did alright."

"You have to chew gum, Fred?"

"Only after I eat."

Alex B. Stone

If you have to chew gum, chew with your mouth shut. That is disgusting, Fred, talking to me with the gum hanging out of your mouth.

I learned to chew gum when we were flying.

That was fifty years ago, Fred.

Dotty, it's difficult for me to get rid of my good habits.

"There, Helen, no more chewing gum."

I always spit my gum out before starting my business day. I want to set a good example for my employees, for my tenants, for the plumber, for the papergoods salesman.

"You know what you ought to do, Fred? Get away from Rockville first chance you get. Take a break, fly down to Sanibel, spend a week in the sun. It will do your arthritis a world of good.

"Angela Lowery still have a thing for you?"

"She likes older men."

"You are not that harmless yet, are you Fred?"

"Who, me?"

"So what are you going to do with the rest of your life?"

"Not much, Helen, not much."

"Doesn't that trouble you, Fred?"

"Okay, I'm going to become a celebrity as soon as my first novel is published. I will give readings, appear on teevee, radio talkshows in New York, Chicago, St. Louis and San Francisco. Helen, I have done enough accomplishing. I have enough just to keep my nineteen twelve office building functional."

"Fred, you are making fun of me. You laugh when I am serious, Fred."

"Laughing about myself, Helen. Not at you."

"If you quit, you could do more for yourself."

"More what?"

"You have talked of going back to Poland to see where we were born, the cemetery where our grandparents are buried."

If I Could Sleep . . .

"It is a potato field. Grandpa's house is a six plex. The farms are gone, the government has them all."

"You could try to get them back. You know about farming."

"I'll become the Jewish absentee landlord of a Polish estate, an exploiter of poor peasant tenant farmers."

"You could teach them about raising hogs. Papa taught you all about hogs."

"JEWISH LANDLORD RETURNS TO RAISE HOGS IN RURAL NOTHERN POLAND."

"That is not what I meant, Fred. You complicate everything. Just a trip to see."

"To see what?"

"What has happened to Sczuczyn since we left."

"Helen, that was sixty eight years ago."

"It was a thought."

"I mean, if you like we could go. You make the arrangements, Helen. I'll pay for the trip.

"You know, I had a very strange dream last night. I saw a fat steer go through a round opening in a wall."

"So, what is that supposed to mean, Fred?"

"I don't know, but I think it has something to do with how we can't see beyond today, can't see our future."

"You should take a sleep aid, cut down on your disturbing dreams."

"I am not disturbed. It's just a dream—a Zen dream, actually . . ."

"I am glad you can share your Zen dreams with me, but whom do you talk to when I am not here?"

"Sometimes I talk to the Rabbi. Not often."

"You don't talk to your friends?"

"Not about personal things. All we do is sit around, complain about taxes. Dreams are personal, aren't they?"

They are my dreams. I wish you love, I wish you shelter from the storm...

"You talking to yourself, Fred?"

"I was humming."

Should I forget you, if I forsake you . . .

Emily! Never!

Look at me, look at me, Papa...

That was a great dive, Emily, great!

"Does anything ever change in the downtown?"

"Not really, Helen. Not in the last twelve years."

Downtown Rockville. Two banks, built in the '20s, each with its own parking lot. A florist. A camerashop. Three office buildings. An Andrew Carnegie library. The postoffice, the city hall, one parking garage and no matter how many old buildings are demolished there are never enough parking spaces.

"I'll park behind the building, we can walk to the bank."

"I know where it is."

Enter the vault through the first double glass door on the right, down the pink Tennessee marble stairs, hold onto the brass handrail, into a small reception area in front of the open door of the safe.

"Good morning, Mr. Stern. I read about your daughter. I am sorry."

"Thank you. My sister, Helen Gordon."

"How do you do, Mrs. Gordon?"

"Helen, do you want to wait for me in the middle cubicle, the one with the open door?"

Close the door and enter. Private, Reserved For Lock Box Holders. The greenglass shade over the singlebulb desklamp shines on two straightbacked mahogany chairs. On the glasstopped table a scissors, white businessenvelopes and a letteropener.

"They know you at the bank."

"I am a frequent visitor."

I have achieved the largest safety deposit box available. This after a wait of ten or more years, an honor bestowed only on the very oldest and finest of the Cream of Rockville business clients.

In the box, on top, in their blue folders, the abstracts. Next the art inventory and appraisals. Then the art library inventory. Under that the wills in plain white envelopes, tied until death with blue ribbon, identified by the names Fred B. Stern, Emily M. Stern.

"Open it, Fred."

"I will."

"Read it."

June 15, 1990

I, Emily Stern, bequeath to my father, Fred B. Stern, who loved me more than I deserved, all my worldly goods, to dispose of as he sees fit.

Emily Stern

Witnessed June 15, 1990. J.J. Carr, V.P. Mountain National Bank, Denver Colorado.

"It's all right to cry, Fred, it's all right."

"There is more, Helen."

PS. Dear Pops,

There was no one else whom I would trust more, no one else who I ever found as caring as you. I do hope I have not burdened you with my things.

Love, Emily

"Emily loved me."

"Did you ever doubt that?"

"Not now."

"Emily bought you a Baume and Mercier watch for your birthday."

"I wasn't talking about things, Helen. I would have exchanged the watch for a ten minute walk, a lunch, two days together, or even for an afternoon alone with Emily. Busy, always too busy. I was too busy, Emily was too busy, Edna is too busy, Edith is too busy. See? I wear the watch Emily gave me.

"I'll make copies of the will, send one to Emily's attorney in Denver, send one to Edith, one to Edna."

"May I have one, Fred?"

"If you wish."

"Emily's will is a love letter to you.

"What are you going to do now, Fred?"

"Go up to my office. Look at the mail, look . . . look at the messages."

"Then what?"

"I go swimming at noon, eat lunch and then I come back to the office for a half an hour or so, then I go home. I'll be home by about four."

"What would you like me to do, Fred?"

"Whatever you like. Sit in the office, write some letters, read the New York Times, walk over to the library. Come back by a quarter to one. I'll take you to lunch anywhere you like."

"Can we go to Denny's?"

"That's not funny, Helen."

If I Could Sleep . . .

"Anything changed in your office since nineteen twelve?"

"No."

Same grey marble wainscoting in the halls, same slate stairs, same crazed ceramic urinals, same walnut doorframes that open into 150 square feet of modernized office space with window airconditioners and radiator steamheat. The south suites still look out over the abandoned railroad. The panorama on the north is of the parkinglots.

"Fred, when are you going to modernize your office?"

On my Scandinavian desk a triptych of photos. Emily on the left, Edith in the center and Edna on the right. Flanking the daughters, their middleaged parents, Dotty and Fred, photographed in blackandwhite in 1966 or '67 by Swanson of Rockville.

"I'll go to the office with you, Fred.

"I know why you never remarried, Fred. I know. I knew why the moment I walked into your home. Now, I am sure of it. Look at your office. Nothing has been changed in fifteen years. The same prints on the wall, Sandzen, Gropper and Rockwell Kent. The artists you admired when you were thirty years old."

"My taste has changed, Helen. I have been buying Marca-Relli and Philip Guston. What is on the wall is the historical beginnings of my art collection. Old isn't bad, new isn't better. Just different."

"Who said that?"

"Fred Stern, your own wonderful dear brother Fred."

"Fred, do you ever think of what your life would have been if you had become a professor of economics? Don't laugh!"

"Economics is a wonderful field. Just no way to earn a living, not in a small midwestern town."

"You would have done so well in academia."

"Only average earnings. I wanted more. Dotty would have been satisfied. I wasn't. She wanted the security. I would have died of boredom and frustration. I wanted success, wealth, travel, art. Wanted to leave something behind me. The world better than I found it.

Maybe it's not everything I hoped for, but it's something, Helen. Dotty knew it, too. She just had a hard time admitting it."

"Now you could remarry. Now you have choices. You earned the choices. You could choose a life of leisure, a bit of fun.

"Tell me I'm right, Fred. You didn't remarry because . . . ?"

"I'll tell you why, Helen. Because I am not an optimist. Dotty and I done good. From where we started, what we accomplished, what we achieved was a miracle. Our history is a history of miracles and how often would there be two miracles in one lifetime? Tell me."

"Why shouldn't there be two miracles? If you can have one, you can have two. Why . . . Oh forget it, Fred! You are too busy to talk to me. You have your nose in your mail already. That's more important. What is so important in your mail that it can't wait for us to finish our talk?"

"Another of our tenants gave notice. The James Company is moving out next month."

Un Azoy Vayter

About Red Heifer Press

Red Heifer Press is an independent press devoted to the publishing and audiopublishing of works of unusual interest and merit in literary fiction, poetry, documentary memoirs, belles lettres, beaux arts, sheet music, scholarship in the Humanities and Torah/Judaica in English. For further information about Red Heifer Press, or to view our growing catalog of fine books and compact discs, please visit our website: www.redheiferpress.com.

Connoisseurs of classical and contemporary music are invited to become acquainted with our musical recording alter ego, Leonore Library of Musical Masters. Leonore is dedicated to the restoration, preservation and dissemination on compact disc of rare and neglected recordings of special musical and historical significance. We are currently engaged, in association with Cambria Master Recordings, in the restoration and reissue of the many outstanding recordings of Jakob and Bronislaw Gimpel. For more information, please visit: www.leonoremusic.com, and www.cambriamus.com.

THIS BOOK WAS PRINTED AND BOUND BY

Sheridan Books, Inc.
613 East Industrial Drive
Chelsea, Michigan